Praise for *Just My Luck*

"I loved this portrait of a young boy struggling to find his role in a family determined not to be defined by their differences. Benny's brave story, told with wry humor, is inspirational." —Ann M. Martin, *New York Times* bestselling author of *Rain Reign*

"In narrator Benny, readers find a resilient and very observant nine-year-old who accepts those around him with their strengths and shortcomings alike. His story is insightful and inspirational." —*Kirkus Reviews*

"McGovern's thoughtful depiction of a family facing difficult situations without fracturing, coupled with a gentle message about not being too hard on oneself, will surely speak to middle schoolers with their own slate of worries." —*Publishers Weekly*

"A heart-filled story of a likable boy who doesn't realize that his natural gifts are recognizable and valued by a supportive family. There are many moments that will ring true to middle grade readers: feeling anxious about friendships, wanting to be noticed, and trying to do the right thing." —*School Library Journal*

"McGovern's observations about ordinary-seeming life and about the people around us, about small acts of kindness and healing and forgiveness, are perceptive and thought-provoking." —*The Horn Book*

"Benny's first-person narrative radiates with exactly the kind of compassion his mother recommends. Like many nine-year-olds, Benny can be guileless in one moment and wise beyond his years in another. Highly recommended for fans of realistic fiction by writers such as Ann M. Martin or Lisa Graff." —ALA *Booklist*

"McGovern writes convincingly about characters trying to figure out how best to live with the complications of a disability, both the person whom it most affects and also those around him or her. Benny's voice deserves to be read aloud in a classroom." —*VOYA*

Also by Cammie McGovern

For Young Readers

Chester and Gus

For Teens

Say What You Will

A Step Toward Falling

JUST MY LUCK

Cammie McGovern

HARPER
An Imprint of HarperCollins*Publishers*

HarperCollins Publishers
Since 1817

Grateful acknowledgment is given to Naomi Shihab Nye for permission to use a selection from her poem "Kindness" from *The Words Under the Words: Selected Poems.*

Just My Luck

For information address HarperCollins Children's Books, a division of HarperCollins Publishers, 195 Broadway, New York, NY 10007.
www.harpercollinschildrens.com

Library of Congress Control Number: 2015938989
ISBN 978-0-06-233066-6

Typography by Aurora Parlagreco
18 19 20 BRR 10 9 8 7 6 5 4 3

❖

First paperback edition, 2017

For Ethan, Charlie, and Henry,
who gave me most of the good lines in here

ONE

MY MOM HAS A THEORY THAT when bad things happen, you should think about someone else's problems and try to help them. Like even if you're losing a soccer game terribly you should try to help the poor guy wearing glasses on the other team who just fell down. Things like that. One problem with Mom's theory is that my older brother George is autistic, which means he can't really think about anyone else, much less help them. The other problem is that ever since this summer and what happened to Dad, I don't think anyone else has more problems than we do.

What happened to Dad this summer wasn't my fault.

The first night that Mom came home from the hospital,

she said this to me, and she's been saying it ever since, which of course makes me feel like it *was* my fault, at least a little bit.

The morning that it happened, Dad asked me if I wanted to go to the high school to work on my bike riding. Which was embarrassing because *I'm in fourth grade now.* Of course I can *ride a bike.* Sort of. I just have a hard time starting. And stopping. It also makes me a little nervous slowing down to make turns.

I wasn't always this way. I could ride a bike when I was in second grade like everyone else. Maybe I kept my training wheels on longer than other kids but eventually I let my dad take them off and I made it up and down the street a bunch of times, Dad jogging next to me, Mom taking pictures. I would have said I was a fine bike rider until the end of that summer when we had a bike parade at our block party. We have twelve kids on our block, most of them younger than us, so every bike was decorated with streamers and pom-poms. Stephanie up the street is a year younger than I am, but she had taped pinwheels to her handlebars, which was such a good idea I was jealous. Especially when I saw how they spun like crazy when she rode fast. All I had for decoration was a few streamers flapping and two balloons tied to my handlebars, but they weren't doing much. Anyone could see Stephanie's pinwheels were going to win, which made me so mad, I pedaled really hard and fast, *bam!* right into a parked car. I flew into the street and the whole bike parade stopped so everyone could get off their bikes and gather around in a circle to see if I was still alive.

I was. Barely.

Afterward Martin, my oldest brother who's in ninth grade now, kept saying it didn't look that bad. "It was a little funny, actually," he said. "Kind of like a sight gag."

He was trying to make me feel better because it wasn't funny at all.

For a long time afterward, I didn't get on my bike. Even when Martin and his friends built a bike jump out of wood planks and cement blocks, I pretended my foot was hurt so I wouldn't have to do it. When they did races up the street, I would say I heard my mom calling me, so no one would ask why I wasn't racing.

The week before school started this year, Dad called me outside to say he had an idea. "I'm going for a run over at the high school. No one will be there. The track there is a great place to practice riding your bike. No curbs to worry about. No cars to run into . . ."

He clapped his hands like coaches do at halftime when their team is losing.

"I don't know, Dad," I said.

I felt bad for him. When he was a boy, Dad went to a prep school where everyone had to wear ties to class and play a sport every season, even if they were terrible at it. "I hated it. I wouldn't wish that on any of you," he always tells us, but sometimes I wonder if he wishes his sons were a little more like the jocks he says he never liked.

Dad has been an assistant coach on all of our soccer teams, which means his hardest job every year has been thinking up new words to describe our performance when he hands out end-of-the-season trophies. "Benny has worked so hard with the skills he has," he'll say. Or "Benny has been trying to reach a new level of playing. This year he almost has." He says these things because at trophy ceremonies you're not allowed to say the truth, which is "Benny hasn't touched a ball in a game once all season." He also can't say, "Benny seems remarkably uninterested in this sport in spite of all the years I've put in as an assistant coach."

I think if Dad had his secret dream come true, he'd have one of us be a surprisingly good athlete so he could stand on the sidelines of games and say, "It didn't come from me! I'm a terrible athlete!"

Instead he has my brother Martin, who plays basketball because this year he's the tallest boy in ninth grade, but even Martin will admit he's a terrible shooter and anyone in their right mind doesn't throw the ball to him. He also has George, who plays in Special Olympics basketball, where it's okay to just carry the ball from one end of the court to the other without dribbling at all. And me, Benny, who can only ride a bike if someone is there to help me start and stop.

"I don't think that sounds like such a good idea, Dad," I told him after he suggested bike riding at the high school track. I don't know if he realized this, but I hadn't ridden my bike once since the bike parade. I'd *walked* my bike places, and when I got there, I *pretended* I'd rode, but I hadn't actually gotten on my bike and pedaled it since my crash.

"It'll be fun," Dad said. "I'll be right there. Running my laps."

The way he said this, I could tell that he *did* know that I hadn't been on my bike in two years. Mom came outside and they looked at each other like they'd talked about it ahead of time. Like they were both really worried about this, which made me feel *terrible.*

"Okay," I said. "I guess I could try."

Mom hugged me right away. "That's wonderful, Benny! We're so proud of you!"

That afternoon, we got out to the track early while it was still deserted, which was lucky because it turned out that I was even worse than I remembered. Walking over, Dad told me there was an old saying about how you have to get right back on your bike when you fall off. "Or maybe that's a horse," he said. "But the point is you shouldn't wait a year to get back onto whatever you fell off of."

That was a nice idea, except the first time I tried pedaling, I veered right off the track and onto the grass. I don't know if this is true for other people, but whenever I fall off my bike, I'm always sure, for about thirty seconds, that I've broken my leg. There are so many bars that could crush a leg that I can never believe it hasn't happened.

I lay there for a while, looking up at sky, waiting to experience what a broken leg feels like. *It's okay,* I told myself. *If it's broken, I won't have to ride this stupid bike again for a long, long time.*

Then came the bad news.

"Looks like you're okay!" Dad said. "Good to go! Right back in the saddle!" He leaned over. His face was a little red from the effort of staying upbeat. "You're okay, right?"

"I think so."

"Super! Why don't I hold the seat while you start pedaling?"

It's embarrassing to be nine years old and have your dad hold your bike seat while you climb on. It's also embarrassing to have him run beside you screaming, "You're veering! You're veering! Make your adjustment!"

But here was the surprise: once I got going, I was fine!

Better than fine! I flew around the track, lightning fast.

I made it around one whole lap while Dad watched me, clapping and cheering. He was right—the track was a great place to practice. I didn't have to worry about running into anything except painted lines on the ground. I got my speed up and practiced staying in between two lines, which was hard, so I gave myself two lanes, which wasn't hard at all.

I couldn't believe how good I was, especially compared to Dad, after he started jogging. Dad didn't really run laps. He shuffled at this strange pace where his legs looked like they were running but old women walked faster. "It's not about speed," he always said, which in his case was certainly true. He looked like he was running backward compared to me.

Poor Dad had to sweat and huff and shuffle to get around the track three times and I lost count after ten. I felt great, like maybe I should become a professional bike rider. Then I saw a woman up ahead on the track, running with her dog. The dog was on a leash, but he liked the inside lane and she liked the outside lane so there was a line stretched like a fence across the track. If I ran into that line, I was sure it would chop me in half, which made me panic and forget how to stop.

I stuck both legs out and yanked the hand brakes, which meant I didn't slow down gradually. My bike stopped but my body didn't. I flew headfirst over the handlebars. I saw the ground, then the sky, then nothing at all.

At the last minute I guess my dad came up behind to help me. His head hit my helmet. Or maybe my head hit his shoulder and he fell back and hit the track. We never figured out exactly what happened. When we got up, a little dazed, he seemed fine. He was more worried about me.

He walked my bike back to the car and drove us home, where he had me lie down on the sofa while he looked up the signs of a concussion, because even though there are three boys in our family, none of us is athletic enough to have ever gotten one.

"Do you feel like throwing up?" he called from his office, where the computer is.

“I don’t think so.”

“Do you feel dizzy or confused or lethargic?”

“What’s lethargic?”

“Tired.”

“Sort of.”

“Do you have double vision or a vague feeling of malaise?”

“What’s that?”

“Feeling gloomy.”

“A little,” I say.

Then—this part is hard for me to think about—while he was still asking my symptoms and reading about concussions on the screen, he slid out of his chair and hit the floor with a thud. I will never forget that sound even if I try to for the rest of my life. Mom heard it, too, and ran into the room. When she couldn’t wake him up, she called out for Martin to please call 911.

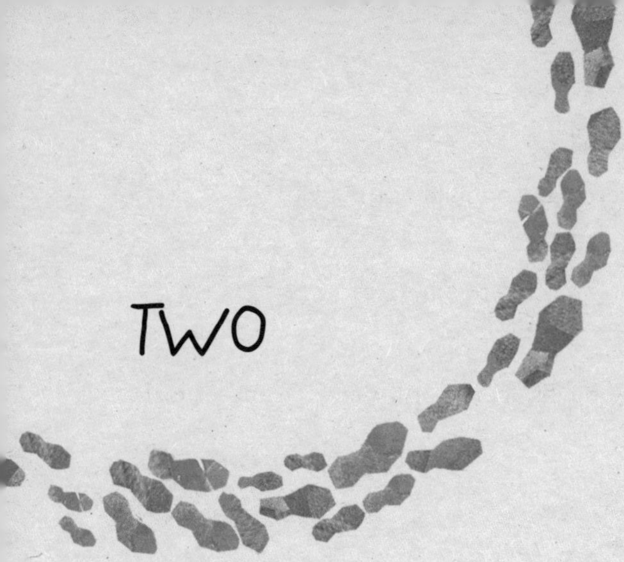

TWO

SINCE THEN, I'VE BEEN TRYING TO think of other people who might have worse problems than we do. For instance, this week I've been wondering if maybe my teacher, Mr. Norris, has problems. Over the summer I was so happy when I found out I was getting Mr. Norris. Out of three fourth grade teachers, he's the one everyone wants because he's funny and dresses a little like one of the kids. He wears jeans and sandals and has curly hair he sticks pencils in and then forgets about. The first few weeks of school he was great. He brought in snacks he'd baked at home using ingredients we were supposed to guess. Usually it was a hidden vegetable like carrots or zucchini. Once he brought in beet bars that he said tasted like brownies, and we all said that was true even if it wasn't. But we didn't care if his snacks didn't taste good. We ate them anyway and acted like they were great. Once Amelia asked for his recipe and then we all asked for it, not because we wanted to make his bars at home but to get our own index card with his handwriting all over it.

Now I realize that's the biggest problem with a teacher like Mr. Norris. Everyone wants him to like them best. Which means Jeremy Johnson—who I have to be best friends with this year because Kenneth, my old best friend, moved to Florida last year—memorizes everything Mr. Norris says to him. The first week of school Jeremy told me, "Mr. Norris thinks I'll probably be in the top math group. Same with spelling. I told him I usually am."

I'm terrible at math and spelling. During the second week, each of us sat alone with Mr. Norris and answered questions so he could figure out which group we belonged in. Judging by what Jeremy said, he aced all his tests.

To me, Mr. Norris just said, "Thanks for trying your best, Benny," which is what teachers say to the kids who get put in slow groups.

Now we've been in the fourth grade for a month and a half, working hard to win compliments from Mr. Norris, but in the last few weeks, I've been wondering if maybe Mr. Norris has a problem. I think about what my mom used to say and wonder if there's some way I might help him.

This whole last week, he's come in late every morning with no pan of baked goods. Today, halfway through math, he realized he hadn't taken attendance or sent the lunch list to the main office. "I'm sorry," he said when a messenger from the main office stopped by for the list. "Seems like I'm late with everything these days."

It's true, I thought. It's hard to explain why he'd be coming to school late when he lives in an apartment complex next door to school. Once at recess he showed us the path he walks to school and said, "Look! No traffic!" Except lately he doesn't walk on his no-traffic path, he drives his car, which is covered in bumper stickers about the importance of recycling and energy conservation.

Jeremy doesn't think this is strange, but I do.

"Doesn't walking conserve more energy?" I say at lunch. "He only lives about two hundred yards away."

"Not if he's running late."

"So why is he always running late?"

"Because maybe he sleeps in. Maybe he's up late playing video games," Jeremy says.

We know he lives alone in his apartment because Charlotte once asked if he was married and he said, "Ah, no. No, I'm not, Charlotte."

The girls thought he sounded sad when he said this and now they want him to wait for them to grow up so they can marry him. The boys don't see his life as sad. We know he has a PlayStation even though he's never mentioned having children, which means he must live the life we all dream of someday, where he can come home from school, eat what he wants, and play video games all night if he feels like it. Which must be great, except lately it seems like maybe it's not.

When I remind Jeremy how Mr. Norris has been late to everything, Jeremy thinks about it and admits he's noticed a few things, too. Like Mr. Norris closing his eyes during Shoshanna's oral book report on *When Zachary Beaver Came to Town*. We're supposed to pick out a theme to talk about in our oral book reports. Supposedly Shoshanna's a really good reader—she always reads thick books, at least—but that day I wondered if maybe she missed something. "The main theme of this book is that Zachary Beaver is really fat," Shoshanna said. "Fatter than any of us will ever be."

I looked over at Mr. Norris to see if he would say anything

and realized he wasn't closing his eyes to listen better, *he was asleep*.

After a while, even Shoshanna noticed and stopped doing her book report. "Mr. Norris?" she said.

Nothing.

"Mr. Norris?" she said again.

Still nothing. I started to panic a little. After this summer, I've learned that bad things can happen really fast. I wondered if someone could die sitting up. A few other people must have thought the same thing, because eventually Seamus held up his hand in front of Mr. Norris's mouth. "Still breathing," he whispered.

We all looked at one another. No one knew what to do. It was like being alone in the house after your parents have left but before the babysitter comes over. You could do anything at all, you just can't think of what.

"That was weird," Jeremy says now, finishing up his lunch. "You might be right. Something freaky is going on with Mr. N."

I lean across the table and tell Jeremy, "I want to figure out what it is." I almost tell him I have some ideas from clues I've noticed, but before I can say what they are, Jeremy's attention has drifted to the stage in our cafetorium.

Our principal, Mr. Wilder, and our assistant principal, Ms. Crocker, are setting up a presentation. There's a bright green poster with a yellow footprint that has *One Footprint at a Time* written on it. They unroll another banner that says *We Are a Community of Helpers* and tape it to a table behind the podium.

Poor Ms. Crocker is terrible at getting things like duct tape to work right. First it sticks to her hands, then to her shirt.

Before Mr. Norris came along, Ms. Crocker was the adult I loved most at school. She wears her blond curly hair piled up like a messy bird's nest on top of her head. The first time I saw Ms. Crocker, she was wearing finger cymbals at the kindergarten welcome circle. She pinged them together until everyone was quiet and then she leaned over her lap and whispered, "I think people hear better when I whisper, don't you?"

No one said anything. We were too busy listening.

After lunch, there's an all-school assembly, which means the tables get pushed back and everyone sits on the floor in rows. We're supposed to sit youngest up front, but in the middle we always get mixed up. Today, my brother George's class sits in front of us even though I'm in the fourth grade and he's in sixth. George is what my mom calls "medium-functioning autistic," which means he isn't high functioning and he isn't low functioning. He can talk, for instance, but a lot of what he says doesn't make much sense. He's a big one for repeating lines that people have said earlier in the day. When he sees me at assembly, he says, "No more water, silly boy."

"Hi, George," I say.

He turns around on the floor to do a new joke I started at home where I brush my teeth with my finger. To be honest, it's not that funny, but this week it's really cracking George up. George is the only one in my family who still laughs at stupid little jokes like this.

He rubs his finger over his teeth to get me to do it.

"No, George," I whisper. "We have to pay attention."

I point to the stage where Ms. Crocker is trying to get her microphone to work. "Can you hear me?" she says. Or at least that's what it sounds like she says. We can't really hear her.

"Turn around!" I tell George. "You'll get in trouble."

He laughs and rocks back and forth, holding his knees. He won't turn around until I brush my teeth with my finger, so I do it quickly.

He laughs so hard he falls over and the girl sitting next to him has to help him up. "You shouldn't laugh so hard, George," she says. "You'll hurt yourself."

George doesn't really have any friends. Instead he has a few girls who act like his mother and tie his shoelaces for him, even though he's in sixth grade. I don't think he likes them that much, but I've never really been sure.

Finally Ms. Crocker gets the microphone to work when Mr. Wilson shows her how to turn it on. She tells us this assembly is about an exciting new program called C.A.R.E. She points to a poster that has a period between each letter, which usually means it stands for something else. I'm right, it does: Cooperation. Accountability. Respect. Empathy.

Ms. Crocker tells us that deep down in our hearts, each of us has these qualities, but sometimes we forget to show them in everyday ways like bending over to pick up litter or lending someone a pen. "Here's the idea," she says. "For two months teachers and staff will be watching you and whenever they see you doing nice things that show your empathy and compassion, they'll write it down on little paper footprints. One step at a time, we'll post these random acts of kindness so everyone can see what a caring community looks like. And because this is all about working together, the class with the most footprints at the end of two months will win a pizza party!"

It's hard to tell, but it seems like maybe this is an idea Ms. Crocker really wanted to do and Mr. Wilson, our principal, didn't. She keeps looking at him nervously while she talks. I know how she feels. Mr. Wilson scares all of us, even though he has a hard time remembering our names and usually calls you "son" if he yells at you in the hall.

Ms. Crocker remembers our names and which buses we ride on, which means everyone likes her almost as much as I do and everyone claps for her C.A.R.E. idea. Ms. Crocker's other problem (besides duct tape and Mr. Wilson) is that sometimes she tries a little too hard, like she does at the end of the assembly when she has us all sing a song with the words on a screen under a bouncing ball.

We show compassion and empathy!
Deep down in our hearts!
We show kindness and cooperation!
Deep down in our hearts!
I said DEEP, DEEP!
I said DOWN, DOWN!
I said deep down in our hearts!

It's not a very good song and it goes on for way too long. Even Ms. Crocker realizes this about halfway through because she laughs and says into the microphone, "All right, people, let's just get through this."

By the end, I'm pretty sure everyone loves Ms. Crocker as much as I do.

Which means we can't help it, we all want to earn footprints and we all want to win the pizza party.

THREE

AFTER THE C.A.R.E. ASSEMBLY, WE GO outside for recess, where Jeremy says he's sorry he can't spend recess with me because a bunch of guys asked him to play soccer. A bunch of guys have definitely *not* asked me to play soccer. If I go over to the field, they'd probably ask me to stand on the side and chase the ball when it goes out. I said yes to that once and learned my lesson when the ball kept going into the pricker bushes that no one else would go near.

I walk over to the swings that are wet and then to the girls who are sitting near the benches playing jacks. Last year it was still okay to play chase games and hide-and-seek with the girls. This year when I asked Amelia and some of the other girls if they wanted to play Outlaw & Posse, Jeremy told me that I should be careful about playing too much with girls. "You start to look like one if you do that," he said.

Today all the boys are playing soccer and not looking over here so I don't care what I look like except I guess jacks takes too much concentration for anyone to answer when I say hi. I don't know what's happening with some of the girls this year. It seems like they've broken into groups. One group is trying to look older and wears fingernail polish and is being mean to the other group, which I don't understand.

Then I notice the sixth graders are outside playing doctor dodgeball, which is like regular dodgeball except after you get hit and die, a "doctor" is allowed to go onto the field and heal you. It's supposed to be like dodgeball only "nicer," but I think kids lying on the ground, lifting their heads and calling, "Doctor! Doctor!" is even scarier than reaching for soccer balls in pricker bushes. I go over to the little kids' playground, where a bunch of big tires are planted sideways for kids to climb on. George has one tire he spends most of his recess in. For a while, the teachers tried to make George play a game with other kids before they let him sit inside his tire and dribble wood chips for half an hour. Then they decided that school was hard enough for George and he should be able to do what he wants at recess.

"Hi, George," I say, standing next to his tire. He laughs and rocks and throws a wood chip at my feet.

Out of everyone in our family I'm usually the best one at getting George to laugh. It's not that hard because he always laughs at the same things. Like finger-brushing my teeth. Or singing "skidamarinky-dinky-dink, skidamarinky-doo."

I climb inside his tire and sit down across from him. I ask what he thinks about Ms. Crocker's C.A.R.E. footprints idea. He doesn't say anything, but he giggles and rocks because he likes having someone in his tire with him. I'm not sure why. I think he likes the echo of voices inside the rubber, which gives me an idea. I lean inside the empty rubber part and sing "skidamarinky-dinky-dink, skidamarinky-doo" so it travels in a half-circle vibration around to George's side.

He laughs and sits up so his ears are inside the sound. When I do it again, he laughs more and claps, so I keep doing it for a while. I say, "No more water, silly boy," into the rubbery echo chamber.

George falls over laughing.

One thing about autism that people might not realize: on the surface it looks like you're bad at everything—like playing games, eating neatly, tying your shoes—but secretly, some autistic kids can be very good at certain things. Like math maybe, except not George. George is terrible at math. Worse than me, even. Martin will ask George a question like "Hey, George, what's two plus two?" because it's funny to see him scrunch up his face, trying hard to think of an answer. Usually after about thirty seconds, Martin will pat him on the shoulder and say, "It's okay, bud. Don't hurt yourself. I'll ask someone else." We don't play very many tricks on George because that would be mean. But sometimes if we're alone in the room, it's a little funny.

No one knows why autistic kids are bad at certain things and good at other things. George can repeat a whole scene word for word from *Pirates of the Caribbean*, but if you ask him a question like "What do you think of C.A.R.E. footprints?" he'll almost never answer. Even if it's an easy question, like "Did you have music today?" or "Did you earn all your stars?" he'll have no idea how to answer. His brain just doesn't understand certain things.

One thing George is really good at is singing. Once our music teacher, Ms. Dunbar, told me he was one of only a handful of students she's had with perfect pitch. Like if she named a note, he could sing it perfectly, no piano needed.

"Not very many people can do that, Benny," she said. That made me feel proud.

But here's the weirdest thing that George can do really well: ride a bike.

The rest of the family might not even realize how good George is because they didn't see what I saw last year. It happened the day Martin and his friends constructed a bunch of ramps to do skateboard tricks on. Mostly, Martin's friends are terrible skateboarders and fell off the ramps on every try. In fact, in two hours no one landed a single jump. Eventually they gave up and all went inside to play video games.

That's when George came out, riding his bike. I don't think he knew I was watching because he was staring so hard at those ramps. He must have been in the garage where he goes sometimes to sit on the lawn mower, which is his second favorite machine after the floor waxer at school. Usually he just stares at the lawn mower, but this time he must have been watching them because he knew exactly what he wanted to do. I almost screamed *No, George! Don't!* when I saw him lining his bike up twenty feet away from the ramp.

And then I watched him take off.

I already knew George was a better bike rider than me.

He's so good he can ride off the street and up onto lawns. I'd even seen him drop off curbs without falling. But I'd never seen him do anything like this: he started pedaling fast and got himself low, his face right over his handlebars. When he got to the jump he pulled everything up—his head, his handlebars, everything. And for three seconds—maybe more—he flew. I could see the sky beneath him, both wheels off the ground.

He had enough time to turn the front wheel one way and then the other, before he landed about ten feet away, without falling.

He looked really surprised and a little scared when I ran over and hugged him. "That was great, George! That was great!" I kept saying. "Do it again!"

But he wouldn't.

He just shook his head and walked his bike back to the garage. By the time we went inside, he didn't want to talk about it. I tried to tell Martin and his friends, but they were playing a video game and not really listening. When I looked over at George, he had his fingers in his ears, which is his way of saying he doesn't want to hear whatever you're saying. I couldn't believe it. I tried a few more times to tell the story, but whenever I did, George started humming or covering his ears.

Maybe it scared him. Maybe he didn't want people to know because he didn't want to have to do it again. In the end, I never told anyone and I started to wonder if maybe I imagined the whole thing—George up in the sky, twisting his front wheel like he was aiming for one cloud and then another. George flying for a second, then landing perfectly.

FOUR

BEFORE THE END OF THE SCHOOL day, I'm surprised: there are already two footprints taped on the wall outside the main office. They're the size of a real kid's foot, with handwritten notes on them.

Tanisha helped put away chairs after music class without being asked, one says.

I liked the way Eric helped a friend who fell down at recess, says another.

That afternoon I go home and tell Mom about the footprints.

"That sounds like a nice idea," Mom says. "You'll probably

get more footprints than anyone." Sometimes Mom says things like this that are completely untrue. Last week, for instance, she said my spelling was fine, better than hers even. Now she says I'm her child who understands "kindness" best, but that's because one of her children is George, who doesn't really understand "kindness" at all, and her other child is Martin, who's standing in the pantry, shaking the last of a box of Cheese Nips into his mouth.

"You want to know how to get a few footprints fast?" Martin says, walking out of the pantry with his face covered in orange crumbs. This year Martin has gotten so tall he can change the lightbulb in his room without standing on anything. Sometimes I see him and I can't believe it—I expect him to be short again like he used to be and he's not. I'm surprised he was listening when I told our mom about the footprints. These days he's usually on his phone or texting and doesn't hear much of what anyone says around him.

"Yes," I say, because I could use all the help I can get. I'm already nervous that Jeremy will get more footprints than me. Jeremy always knows when teachers are watching him. He'll plan his nice things and do them then.

"After lunch, go around picking up trash and then, before

you throw it away, say 'This wasn't mine,' really loud so someone hears you."

It's not a bad idea.

"Ms. Champoux hates litterers," he says. Ms. Champoux is the school secretary, who we all love because her name sounds like "shampoo" even though, when you look at the name plate on her desk, none of the letters are the same. She monitors lunch three times a week and Martin's right: she hates when people don't pick up their trash.

I try it the next day but realize too late about six other people have beaten me to it. "What's this—is everyone suddenly on a clean kick?" Ms. Champoux says, shaking her head. I can't bring myself to say, *I don't really care about trash. I'm just hoping for a footprint.*

It turns out I'm not the only person who feels this way. At math time in the afternoon, Rayshawn raises his hand and asks if Mr. Norris needs any help sharpening pencils.

"No," Mr. Norris says. "Thank you, though, Rayshawn. I like how everyone is trying to be a helper." This morning Mr. Norris was on time to school, but he looks like he's wearing a shirt with food stains on it. I want to point this out to Jeremy, but he's too busy looking for ways to earn a footprint.

Jeremy spends most of lunch talking about everything he's done. He's held a door for Ms. Dunbar, who had her hands full. At recess he brought in a girl's jacket and put it in the lost and found. "The hard part is getting someone to *see* you doing this stuff," he says. "I was standing there forever, holding this pink jacket by the lost and found. Finally I just had to put it in even though no one was looking."

I'll admit this: last spring, when I found out my old best friend, Kenneth, would be moving, I tried to plan ahead and get someone besides Jeremy to be my best friend. I wanted to find a person who likes playing Legos as much as I do. Kenneth and I had a lot of great Lego battles. Sometimes they went on for hours. My mom said it would be okay after he moved, that we could still keep in touch over Skype, but I knew it would feel stupid—both of us staring at the computer, holding up new minifigs we'd gotten.

So last spring I invited Rayshawn over to my house after school. Rayshawn is funny and nice and has a great smile. I knew he would be a long shot as a best friend because he's better at every single sport than me, including nonsports like tabletop football, which you play by flicking a folded-up triangle of paper with your fingers. Still, I invited him because sometimes he laughed pretty hard at my jokes.

I thought maybe that would be enough to start a friendship, but once he got to my house, I couldn't think of anything funny to say. He spent the first ten minutes looking through the cupboards for something to eat. "This all you have?" he said, holding up a loaf of wheat bread.

"Pretty much," I said, thinking, *This might be the shortest friendship in history.*

Then he shrugged, found butter, and said, "I make great toast. Wait'll you taste my toast."

By great toast, I think he meant *a lot of butter with a small layer of bread.*

Which was great, I have to admit.

After we finished our food, though, it was hard to think of anything else to do. Fifteen minutes of looking at my Lego collection was enough for Rayshawn. After that, we went outside and played basketball in my driveway. He killed me twice in knockout and horse and finally he said, "Maybe we should just do free throws," which was nice of him actually. I guess it's not that much fun always winning.

"Sure," I said, "let's just do free throws."

And then a funny thing happened. After twenty tries, I started getting the ball in. Once, twice, three times in a row. We played that if you made it, you kept shooting, so

I had the ball for five minutes straight. Finally I missed on purpose because I was so nervous about how much longer I could keep up my shooting streak.

In the end, we didn't have a bad time, but it didn't feel like anything either one of us wanted to repeat. It's tiring to pretend you like something like basketball. It feels a little like smiling the whole time you're watching a play that your grandmother bought tickets for because you're old enough now to "appreciate Shakespeare."

You wish you could say, *No, I'm really not.*

You wish you could ask your grandmother, *Are you old enough to understand all that?*

But instead, you just smile and feel tired afterward. That's what hanging out with Rayshawn felt like.

If I was friends with Rayshawn, I would climb about twelve rungs up the cool ladder, I'm pretty sure. This year it seems like maybe Rayshawn wouldn't mind being my friend. He still laughs pretty hard at my jokes, and sometimes he laughs when I'm not really joking. Like when I pointed out to Mr. Norris that a three-day weekend was too long for our meat-eating plant to go without meat, Rayshawn shook his head and said, "You're a funny guy, you know that?"

I laughed like maybe I *was* joking about the plant, which I wasn't. It *is* a long time. Supposedly those plants are meant to eat every forty-eight hours. Then I smiled to show Rayshawn I'm not that weird and I don't plan my life around the classroom Venus flytrap.

The only problem with moving up the cool ranks is that it can be a big mistake if you're not really a cool person. It can mean sitting at a lunch table and laughing at stories when you have no idea at all what's funny about them.

It can also make you nervous all the time about being found out.

Last spring, I also tried inviting Keith over once. Keith is shy and never talks much at school, so I thought maybe he'd be fun, but it turned out, no, he was pretty shy away from school, too. When I asked what he liked to do in his free time, he said, "Nothing much, except making paper flowers is okay."

"Paper flowers?" I said.

A babysitter showed him how, with pipe cleaners and tissue paper. "They came out really nice," he said.

There isn't much anyone can say to something like that. You can try, "Great." And "I'd like to see them sometime."

I said both of those things and then we were quiet for the next three hours until his mom showed up.

After that I decided I should probably stick with Jeremy as a best friend for now. Except for being a bragger, Jeremy isn't so bad. The only reason I didn't want to be friends with him in the first place was that I went over to his house once in second grade and had a terrible time. He got mad if I touched any of his already-built Lego things. He kept saying those were for display only, not for play. He said if you play with your Lego after you build it, you can't eBay sell them later when you've outgrown Lego. Or you can, but they're worth less.

After we spent an hour in his room not playing with his toys, his mom made us cream cheese on graham crackers, which I'd never had before. I was scared if I tried it, I might get that gagging thing where food gets stuck in my throat and I accidentally throw up. So I said I wasn't hungry but could I please have a banana?

Jeremy laughed at me for about an hour after that. He said it proved I *was* hungry which meant I was lying.

After I got home, I told my mother no more playdates with Jeremy. She said fine except we had to invite him to our house once since he'd invited me to his. So Jeremy came to my house and spent about fifteen minutes outside George's door listening to him talk to himself, which is what George does every day after he gets home from school. Usually it's a mash-up of things he's heard during the day and lines from his favorite movies. It never makes much sense. Usually we pretty much ignore George talking to himself. Jeremy didn't, though. After he stood outside George's door for a while, he came into my room and asked if I thought George was trying to communicate with aliens.

I said, "I don't think so. Sometimes people with autism talk to themselves, that's all."

"No," he said. "There has to be a reason. I think he's sending messages back to a mother ship or something."

"What mother ship?"

"Exactly. That's what I'm asking. What mother ship?"

That night at dinner I asked my mom and dad what he was talking about. "That's terrible," Mom said. "I'm not going to make you have Jeremy over again."

"But what's a mother ship?"

"It's a horrible, mean thing to say about your brother."

Afterward Mom said that Jeremy was probably insecure, which meant that deep down he didn't feel good about himself, which was why he always had to win at Uno and every other game he plays. Back then, if he didn't win, his face got really red and sometimes he cried.

Now that we're in fourth grade, Jeremy seems like he's changed a lot. Earlier this year, he saw me talking to George on the playground and he came up to me afterward. "Sorry about that thing I said about your brother when I came over to your house," he said.

Even though I pretended to be confused, like I didn't know what he was talking about, we both knew. "It's okay," I said. "He *does* talk like an alien sometimes." That was the first day we ate lunch together this year. George was sitting on the other side of the cafeteria with his aide, Amanda. She was trying to get him to talk to other kids while he ate.

"I think it's kind of cool, actually," Jeremy said. "I like the way your brother talks."

This is the confusing thing about Jeremy. He can also be sort of nice sometimes. Like the other day I got pulled out of class to go to a special room to work on my reading and writing, which was pretty embarrassing. The notice came from the main office on an orange slip of paper and there were only two—one for me and one for Olga, who is a nice girl, but wears thick glasses and is legally blind. I'm not sure what that means because she's not *blind* blind, but her eyeballs shake when she tries to focus on small things (like books) and I think if she ever tried to drive that would definitely be illegal.

I felt terrible, leaving the room with Olga while everyone else was getting ready for book groups, but afterward Jeremy was really nice about it. He said I was lucky, that all they did was talk about a boring book called *The Hundred Dresses*. "If you think one dress is boring, try a hundred," he said. "I wish *I* could have left."

Since then, he's been pretty nice about not pointing out a lot of things like how he always gets 100 percent on spelling tests, and I've never gotten better than 70 percent. Or how he's already in the eights group for multiplication and I'm still back in the twos and threes.

I've always been bad at spelling, which I would have said was my worst subject, but that was before multiplication came along. It turns out, I'm even worse at multiplication. To me it seems like the multiplication tables are just random numbers that were made up to test kids' memories. They seem to have no point, even though teachers keep saying there are lots of practical applications for multiplication. Then they give an example like what if six kids bring eight apples each to a Halloween party, how many do they have in all? Hello? If anyone's at a bad Halloween party like that, they've got plenty of apples and not enough candy. (When I whispered that joke to Jeremy, he laughed pretty hard.)

I don't know why multiplication is so hard for me. I know most of the other kids learned it in third grade. For me, it's like the numbers slip around in my brain and get mixed up. I'll have some answers one week and then forget them the next. Mom got me a computer game where you can shoot a cannon at a bunch of birds every time you get three multiplication facts right in a row. I fly through the twos and scare all the birds and then I get to threes and fours and the birds sit there forever because I can never get three right in a row and I never get the chance to take another shot.

Sometimes I wonder if there's something wrong with my brain that no one is saying because we have enough problems to worry about with George and now my dad. Once I asked my mom and she said, it's okay, everyone learns differently, at their own pace. "There's no law that says every fourth grader has to know the whole times tables by heart," she said.

Except there is, sort of.

Maybe that's why I want to get a footprint so much. It's like ever since I started fourth grade, I spend every day learning new things I'm bad at. I think about what my mom said, that I understand kindness better than my brothers. I don't know if that's true, but I'd sure like to find *something* I'm good at.

FIVE

"I WOULDN'T WORRY ABOUT FOOTPRINTS," Rayshawn says over lunch. "I don't think Mr. Norris is giving them out to *anybody*."

Jeremy and I both look at each other. We're probably trying harder than anyone else and we both know this isn't true. There are about forty footprints up in the hallway now, at least three of which are in Mr. Norris's handwriting, all for the kids I would consider the worst behaved in our class. Like Samuel, who is so fidgety he gets a bumpy plastic cushion to sit on at his desk. And Emma T., who has a little problem with taking things from other children and pretending she has no idea how stuff got into her backpack. Once she stole a dollar fifty from the milk money envelope. When Mr. Norris asked if anyone knew anything about the missing money, she cried and said it was accidentally in her pocket. She might have jail waiting for her in the future, but for now she has a footprint thanking her for cleaning up some paint that spilled in art class.

When I point this out, Jeremy has an explanation. "He *has* to do it for those kids. They get nothing but threes and fours on their report cards."

At our school we don't get grades on our report cards, we get numbers between one and five. Jeremy gets all ones on his report card except for a few twos in subjects he doesn't care about like cooperation and PE. I get numbers that are so far in the middle it's hard for my parents to remember which end we're aiming for. "Wait, is five the best or one?" my mom always asks because looking at my report cards, it's hard to tell.

"Those kids have *nothing else,*" Jeremy says. "I mean seriously. Look at them."

I don't know if Jeremy has forgotten who he's talking to. Or if he's forgotten that this morning another orange notice came from the main office and now I'm getting pulled out of class to work on math, too. This means Olga and I might as well get married we've walked down so many hallways together at this point.

When that notice came, people were busy. It's possible Jeremy didn't even see me leave. I keep hoping he didn't. I'm not sure how many embarrassing things I could expect him to be nice about.

I want to be great at something. That's all.

Martin used to be like me—not such a great athlete, not such a great student—then he got tall enough to make the basketball team. When I tell Mom this, she reminds me that Martin used to be terrible at basketball. "He had to work hard just to make it on the team. Don't you remember the summer before seventh grade when he was out there every day for three months, practicing free throws? You have to choose something and work at it. Look around. Find something you're passionate about."

Mom is a big one for saying we need to find our passion. "I don't care what it is, just as long as it's not video games." The thing is, I *do* have a passion but it's sort of screen related, so Mom rolls her eyes and acts like it doesn't count. I like making short videos with my Lego minifigs. I started doing it with Kenneth two years ago. At first they were terrible. The stories didn't make sense and you could see our fingers moving the minifigs around. Then we worked on it and learned there's a lot of great special effects you can get using stop-motion photography.

Now that Kenneth is gone, I make the movies on my own and I have about three really good ones so far. I'll have two minifigs walk toward each other, holding their light sabers. Then I have them get in a fight. Sometimes heads will roll or arms will come off. My best one has a great joke. Just before a battle starts, Senator Palpatine goes to the bathroom right next to Count Dooku's fort. Dooku turns his head and looks right into the camera like *Can you believe this guy?* And when Palpatine walks away, the Lego base plate is all yellow.

I've showed a few people and they can't believe how well it works. Martin thinks I should post it on YouTube, but I'm not ready for that yet. I don't want strangers making comments on my movies. I can just picture Jeremy saying something like, "This is pretty good, but you can tell a fourth grader made it."

I don't need that.

Plus, I haven't made a new Lego movie since Dad's

accident this summer. Not that anyone has said I shouldn't, it just seems wrong to have Dad sleeping in the next room while I make movies about Lego minifigs knocking each other's heads off.

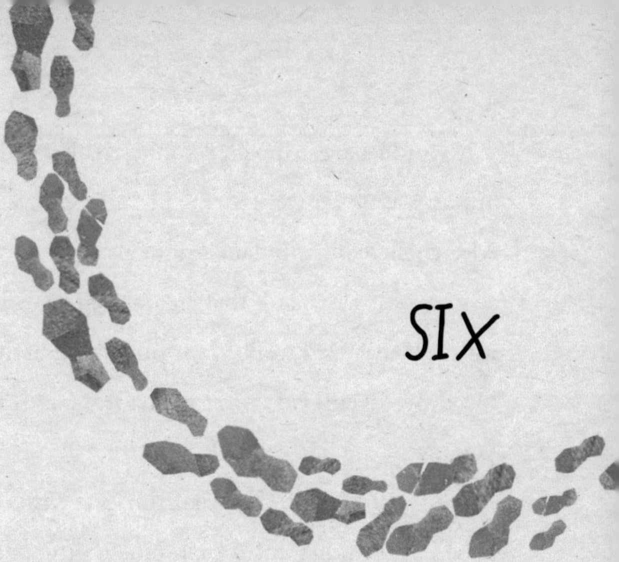

SIX

AFTER DAD WENT TO THE HOSPITAL in an ambulance, it took a long time to figure out what had happened. Mom stayed at the hospital with him all day and called us every hour to say they were still doing tests and didn't know what was going on. That night she finally came home to tell us in person because she didn't want to tell us over the phone. The first thing she said was, "This isn't Benny's fault."

Then she explained: Dad had an aneurysm, which meant a blood vessel started leaking in his brain. It could have ruptured with even less of a bump, the doctor said. "Some people live for years with these things and then walk through a doorway that's too low and suddenly they've got a brain bleed."

It would have happened sooner or later, the doctor said, and in a way we were lucky, because we were all there and Mom called an ambulance right away.

So it wasn't my fault that an ambulance came and it wasn't my fault that Dad went in for surgery right away to stop the bleeding. Even Dad said it wasn't my fault the first time he saw me in the hospital.

We were all scared to see him that visit, but I was surprised. He didn't look that much different. Just thinner and pale and dressed in one of those hospital nightgowns. It was hard to know what to do the first time we visited him because he was attached to wires and machines that we weren't supposed to touch. Of course George touched everything because he can't help himself, so Mom got mad and told him to sit in a chair in the corner. Instead he went into the bathroom and opened all the cupboards in there.

"Maybe it's best to keep this short," Dad said in his soft, croaky voice.

I wanted to cry but I couldn't. On the way there, Mom said whatever we did, crying would be the worst thing because it would make Dad feel worried about how we were all holding up. She said it as a warning to George because he cries so easily sometimes.

On the drive home from that visit, Mom said it was fine to cry now, but only she did. I didn't feel like it anymore. I was too scared that if I started to cry, I'd never stop. George pressed his cheek to the window so he could see his breath and Martin sat in the front seat next to our mother and stared ahead, like he was trying to be the father of the family now.

By the time Dad came home from the hospital, Mom had stopped saying it wasn't my fault and had started saying how lucky we were. Lucky that Dad opened his eyes after surgery and squeezed her hand. Lucky that he walked for the first time three days after surgery. Lucky that he could talk even if he didn't always make sense.

Every time she said it, our dog, Lucky, looked up like maybe she was going to get a treat because we were talking about her so much.

"It just could have been so much worse," Mom said. She'd seen terrible things at the hospital, like people who had been there for months and were still learning how to swallow food again. People who would never walk. People who would drool for the rest of their lives. "Some of the other families couldn't believe your dad was talking the same week he had surgery." She looked over at Lucky, who was back asleep.

We got Lucky the year I was born, which means I'm still a kid but she's very old. "We are *very lucky,*" she whispered, so she wouldn't wake poor Lucky. This might have been true, but the more Mom said it, the more I wondered how unlucky she felt.

First with George, then with Dad.

Because Dad's accident happened at the end of August, a lot of our friends weren't around. After Dad came home from the hospital and school started, a few people found out, but Mom didn't call anyone and tell them what was going on. She kept saying she wanted to wait until we had a better idea of how Dad was doing.

The only friend our age who has been over to the house since the accident is Lisa, Martin's girlfriend, who he started dating last spring. The thing about Lisa is that she's so pretty it's confusing to stand next to her. It's like standing next to the sun. You get all hot and sweaty. No one—including Martin, I'm pretty sure—understands why she chose him to be her boyfriend.

The first time they went out, he brought me along because he was afraid he wouldn't be able to think of enough things to talk about. He told her our mom had made him babysit at the last minute, which made me mad (because she hadn't) but I could also see why he was so nervous: Lisa is beautiful. Her hair is long and blond and almost down to her waist. Her eyes are super blue, like someone colored them in with a cerulean crayon.

Then it surprised me. Right from the beginning, she was really nice and asked me lots of questions. She told me I *had* to get Mr. Norris for fourth grade. "He was my favorite teacher ever!" she said, putting her hand over her heart like it might break just thinking about him. "He's so nice and fun and really inspiring. He keeps these lemon drops in his desk and if you do something special, he calls you up to his desk and gives you one." She made him sound magical. "Some days he doesn't follow a schedule at all. He'll say 'Let's go for a hike, kids, and see what we can find.' Then everyone brings their nature journals outside and hikes in the woods between the apartments and the school."

By the time we walked into Barnes & Noble that day, it felt like she was talking to me more than Martin. She asked what I was reading "these days," like we were old friends who talked about books all the time. She said she knew it sounded childish but her favorite books were still the Little House on the Prairie series that she read when she was in

Mr. Norris's class. "I just love them," she said.

"Oh I know. I love those, too," I said, even though I'd never read them. I knew the stories because our mother used to make us watch the old TV show if she thought we were ruining our minds with too many cartoons.

"I love how they're all so happy at Christmas even though they only get a candy cane and an orange."

"Yeah," Martin said, trying to get in on the conversation. "I love that, too."

Suddenly it was like Martin and I were in a competition. I wanted to tell her that Martin's Christmas lists were twenty items long, everything electronic. I wanted to tell her that he had to work hard to keep those lists under three hundred dollars. I didn't though. I looked at Lisa and knew that if I was on a date with her, I'd probably say anything, too.

Martin never held her hand that day but he took every chance he could to touch her elbow. At the end of the date, I watched from Mom's car as he touched both her elbows and kissed her on the cheek.

Two weeks later, Martin invited Lisa over for dinner. I was all set for her to forget everything we'd talked about and then she came in the family room where I was pretending to read *Little House in the Big Woods* and said, "Oh my gosh, that's my favorite one, Benny! What part are you on?" She leaned over and looked even though I tried not to let her see. "Oh, the first page! That's great—that means you have all the best parts to go."

She told me a few of the good parts and then she really surprised me. She whispered, "I'm a little nervous about this dinner. Maybe you can tell me what I should talk about."

I couldn't believe it. Had Martin not told her how weird our family was? "You can talk about anything," I said. "That's what George does."

"I haven't met George," she said. Then I could tell: that's why she was nervous.

"He's okay," I said and then I thought about it. "I mean, no, he's actually not okay, but you don't have to worry about him."

She laughed like I'd made a really funny joke and put her arm around me. It felt a little weird actually. Like she was *really* nervous about George or something. "Thank you, Benny. Martin's right. You're a great little brother."

That was all before Dad's accident. Lisa was away at horseback riding camp when the accident happened, but I still remember the day she came back. Dad was in the hospital and Mom was exhausted and none of us knew what was going to happen, but seeing Lisa again, tan and smiling and hugging us all, it felt like everything was going to be okay.

Mom gave her an extra big hug and invited her to stay for dinner. Then Mom looked at the stove and realized we were having hot dogs. "Oh well, that's embarrassing, but stay anyway. It's nice to have you back, Lisa. You're like family and we need family around."

Lisa loved hearing that, I could tell. She looked at Martin and then at me. "Of course, Mrs. Barrows. I'd love to."

I still remember the way Mom laughed that night. Not completely like her old self, but almost. In the old days, Mom and Dad loved having people over for barbecues and last-minute dinners. I could tell Mom wanted to be her old self like that, but I could also tell she wasn't sure if it was okay with Dad in the hospital. So with Lisa, she tried it and everyone was happy. Martin was, I know. He made Mom laugh a lot that night. Even George surprised us. After dinner was over, he asked Lisa if he could clear her plate for her. No one had ever heard him ask someone that before. Usually we take turns clearing the table and if it's his turn, he just does it, whether you're done eating or not, so sometimes you have to scream, "George, I'm not finished!"

But that night, he asked her, "Lisa, may I clear your plate?"

He sounded so normal, it made us all stop talking for a minute. Like each of us wondered for a second if George had been playing a joke his whole life, pretending to be autistic. After he took her plate and she thanked him, he walked it over to the sink and put it down. Then he started bouncing around and flapping his hands like his usual crazy self. "There we go," Mom said, like she'd been holding her breath, wondering what was going on.

The next time Lisa came over, it didn't go so well.

In fact, it went much, much worse. Dad was home from the hospital by then and he'd stopped wearing a bandage around his head because the doctors said his wound would heal faster that way. We'd gotten used to the weird way his head looked, completely shaved with a Frankenstein scar down the front of his forehead. It was scary at first—especially when you looked at it and thought about the word *staples*—but if you stared at it for long enough, it got a little better. Or at least you got used to it.

Maybe that's why we forgot to tell Dad to put on a hat before he came out to say hi to Lisa. We were standing in the living room and Mom came in and asked if it was okay and we all said, "Yeah sure! Come on out, Dad!"

Maybe we were all thinking: How bad could it be? He's

home now and still his old self, except maybe he sleeps more and moves slower. Then he came into the living room and he got confused. Like he'd been told Lisa was there but he forgot who Lisa was. Because he walked over to her and put his arms around her and wouldn't let go.

"It's so good to see you," he said, touching her hair, still hugging her with his eyes closed.

After a long time, Martin said, "Ah . . . Dad?"

Lisa looked terrified. "Mr. Barrows?"

"You should stop hugging her now, Dad," Martin said.

We'd never seen Dad do anything like this before. We'd never seen him hug any woman except our mom and our grandmas and we'd never seen him hug either of them this long.

Finally Mom said, "Brian, sweetheart?"

His eyes stayed closed. He looked like he'd fallen asleep with his head on Lisa's shoulder, his mouth and nose buried in her long blond hair.

Then Lisa shocked us all. *"Get him off of me!"* she screamed and shoved him really hard. Mom had to catch him to make sure he didn't fall down.

The whole thing was terrible. Lisa ran into the bathroom, crying. George bounced around in circles, which is what he does when he gets nervous. I stayed in the living room and could tell Dad had no idea what had just happened.

Since then, we've never really talked about that day. How Lisa left a few minutes later without staying for dinner and Mom made us all sit down and eat anyway, even though she was crying, too, by then. I think we were all so embarrassed we didn't know what to say, even after Lisa was gone and it was just us.

In the old days, our dad was one of the reasons friends liked coming over to our house. He followed which sports Martin's friends played and always asked them about it. He also didn't mind spending ten minutes trying a new video game. Then Mom would walk by, roll her eyes, and he'd pass the game console to one of Martin's friends. "Just changing the batteries!" he'd say to Mom, which was one of their inside jokes.

They used to have a lot of jokes like that.

Now it's hard to tell if he remembers their old jokes. He'll start to say something that sounds like one and then he'll forget the word he was looking for. Or he'll fall asleep in his chair, which happens a lot. At first we tried to wake him when it happened, especially if we were all in the room and it wasn't close to bedtime. Now Mom closes her eyes and shakes her head. "Let him sleep," she'll say.

Lisa hasn't been back to the house since that terrible dinner, even though she and Martin are still going out. I don't blame her exactly, because none of us have invited anyone over. Even when Rayshawn mentioned coming over to my house and said that he wouldn't mind making toast again sometime, I had to say, "Yeah, we'll see."

I don't think I could risk having Rayshawn come over. Dad might come out and shake his hand, but he also might follow him around patting his Afro. Every day Dad surprises us by seeming like his old self for a little while and then, just as quickly, he'll seem like a child again or else someone we've never met.

"Give him time," Mom keeps saying. "It takes a long time for a brain to heal. He'll come around, though. I know he will."

Even though she says this, I notice she never invites her old friends inside either. These days more of them stop by to see how we're doing or bring us a dinner, but Mom always talks to them out on the porch. She tells them Dad is napping, otherwise she'd invite them in.

I know for a fact that she's said this when Dad is inside, not napping at all, but watching TV. Which he does a lot.

Usually he watches cooking shows and whatever comes on afterward. Sometimes we'll get home from school and find him sitting on the sofa, watching nothing. It's scary and it's the main reason I never invite my friends over here. Not Rayshawn, who is cooler than I'll ever be, and definitely not Jeremy, who I'm pretty sure is starting to have some doubts about being friends with me at all.

SEVEN

I KNOW I'M PROBABLY THINKING TOO MUCH about who my friends should be. Maybe it's easier than thinking about Dad or remembering how he sometimes felt like my best friend, especially after Kenneth moved away last spring. Dad used to like coming in my room at the end of the day to sit on the floor and look at my Lego set-ups. Because I combine a lot of different sets into bunkers and fortresses, it changes all the time. Some of my designs can be very complicated but also very cool—with elevators and weapon storage units and sleeping quarters for twenty people. Some nights Dad would study everything I'd done and then say, "Do you mind?" and change one little thing.

He'd usually be right, whatever he did. He'd say, "I'd

like the guards on patrol to have easier access to the watchtower," and he'd move a little staircase. Mom can come in and say, "Oh, Benny, it's beautiful!" but she could never do something like that.

Before the accident, it felt like having a best friend didn't matter so much. Now it's different. If Dad isn't Dad anymore, I kind of need someone who can look at my Lego setups and know what needs adjusting. I just do.

I may not be the only one having friendship problems. I used to think all the girls at school were friends and got along well enough to have big sleepovers with six or seven girls, where they all stayed up all night, scaring each other and laughing. Now I've found out they have separate sleepovers, where they make up mean lists ranking the other girls by how much they hate them. It seems like they've divided into two groups that aren't allowed to be friends with each other anymore. One group is the sporty girls, who talk about soccer practices and swim teams, and the other group is the girls who care about their clothes and matching their socks with their headbands. They're also the ones who've started wearing fingernail decals and rubber-band bracelets. And even though we're all trying to be nice and earn footprints these days, it hasn't changed how they've been acting toward one another.

Thursday afternoon, I ask Olga what she thinks about all this. I suppose I'm interested because I'm trying to figure out what the boy groups are and where I fit in. If there are any groups, I'm pretty sure I don't belong to one. I don't know if boys have group sleepovers. I've never been to one, if they do.

Recently, walking down the hall with Olga has gotten to be a little more fun, which is lucky because I do a lot of it. When we're alone, she sometimes laughs so hard her glasses slip down her nose and fall off. Then she always screams at them, "Argh! You glasses!" which makes me laugh. Today when it happens, she picks her glasses up off the floor, leaves her hair in front of her face, and puts her glasses on over her hair. One great thing about Olga is she doesn't care about looking silly or weird. She also doesn't care about getting paint on her clothes in art class or dirt on them at recess. In third grade, when boys and girls still played tag and hide-and-seek together, she was always the girl who found the best hiding spots. Mostly because she didn't mind getting muddy and the other girls did.

Now she says she doesn't understand what's going on with the other girls either. "They make up these stories about each other. I think it's pretty dumb."

That's when I realize, I don't know which group Olga is part of. Sometimes she eats with the sporty girls but mostly she doesn't. When I ask who she eats lunch with, she says, "No one, usually. Mr. Norris lets me eat lunch in the classroom and then I go to the library." She says this like it's nothing. "I told him the lunchroom has gotten a little too cliquey for me—recess too, sometimes."

Clique is a new word we all learned last year. Now even though everyone pretends to hate the cliques, I've never heard of a girl *not* trying to be in one. "What do you do in the library?"

She looks at me sideways. "Read mostly. Sometimes I talk to the librarians. It's not that weird. I'll go back to the cafetorium when all these girl fights die down. I just don't like watching all that. Mr. Norris says he doesn't blame me."

I can hardly believe it. Here I am, worrying every day about who I should eat lunch with, and it's never occurred to me: *I could just skip it altogether.*

Then I remember there's something a little unbelievable about this. "You go to the library *to read*?" I say.

She laughs and stops walking because her glasses have slipped again. "You're right, I don't read. I'm working on a comic book series. The library has this computer program where you can do graphic design that's partly your own art and partly the software. It comes out looking pretty good. The librarian says when I'm done with the whole series, we can make copies and put them on the shelf so anyone who wants to can check them out."

"That's great," I say, even though I'm thinking: *Can a legally blind person really make a comic book?*

Then I think, *So what if she can't?*

Hearing all this makes me admire Olga. I've never had the guts to tell Jeremy about my Lego movies mostly because I care about them too much to have him make fun of them, which is what he'd probably do. Not definitely, but probably.

When we get back to the classroom, everyone is supposed to be working on math, but Mr. Norris isn't even there, so most people are drawing pictures or doing other things. "Where is Mr. Norris?" I whisper to Jeremy.

"Who knows?" He shrugs. Jeremy is working ahead in the math book. He says he wants to be able to start algebra before he gets to middle school. I don't even know what algebra is. "He just disappeared. I think he got a phone call or something. One more example of Mr. Norris being a freak case."

EIGHT

WHEN THE LETTER CAME IN THE mail over the summer saying I got Mr. Norris for fourth grade, Lisa was the first person I told. It was before the accident, so Mom and Dad were both at work. Lisa was in the family room, reading a magazine while Martin took a shower upstairs. "I did it! I got him!" I said, holding my letter.

Then I couldn't believe it: Lisa started to cry.

"That's so great, Benny. I'm so happy for you." She wiped away a tear moving down her cheek. "Don't mind me. I'm just jealous. I wish I was starting fourth grade again. With a whole year of Mr. Norris to look forward to."

Jealous? I thought. I didn't understand. Why would someone who was in high school and was pretty and really popular want to go back to fourth grade?

"I just remember being really happy in fourth grade," she said. "That's all. It's great being a kid. You shouldn't try to hurry through it."

I didn't want to say it, but she sounded a little like one of my grandparents.

After that, she made it her special project to get me ready for Mr. Norris. "Oh, Benny, I forgot about this," she said in late July, before she went away to camp. "He also does this thing called Crazy Hair Backward Day where everyone wears their clothes backward and their hair forward or just really weird. He put his in a million little ponytails. It was so funny!" She laughed at the memory.

After Lisa told me all her happy memories from fourth grade, I think maybe my expectations got raised too high. The first few days of school, I kept waiting for something magical to happen, like she had described. For Mr. Norris to come to school dressed as Paul Revere or some other historical figure we were studying. Lisa's year, apparently he came as Benjamin Franklin and spent the whole morning asking children to explain what all the modern inventions around the classroom were. Lisa said it was hard work pretending he was really Ben Franklin and not Mr. Norris, but after he explained all his inventions to them, they got the point—that a lot of things we still use today are based on ideas Ben Franklin thought of. "He's a *great* actor," Lisa said. "He loves reading aloud and he's super good at it. Our year, he read *The Indian in the Cupboard* and he used different voices for all the toy people that came to life. It was hilarious!"

Even in the beginning of this year when he seemed less distracted, I kept expecting him to do the things Lisa talked about. He'd bring in a tray of beet brownies and I'd wonder about the lemon drops. Or he'd start reading *So B. It,* a book about a normal girl with a mother who seems autistic, and I'd think, *Why is he reading this? Why not something fun with plastic Indians coming to life?*

That's why it's been hard for me to tell if there is something *really* wrong with Mr. Norris or if I just expected too much. This week, though, I'm paying closer attention and I notice a few more unusual things about Mr. Norris.

His fingernails seem longer than they should be. Maybe he plays guitar like my uncle Hank, but Mr. Norris has never mentioned this and usually with guitar players, they have only one hand with long fingernails.

He hasn't shaved in a while, which makes him look a little like my dad after a week in the hospital.

Today, during reading time, his voice got very hoarse. At first I thought he was acting the voice of some new character, the way Lisa described, but that wasn't it. The *story* was making him hoarse, like he was almost going to cry.

At lunch I ask Jeremy if he noticed this and he says no. "Why would Mr. Norris *cry* because of a *book*?"

I tell him I don't know but it seemed like he was about to.

"You're crazy," Jeremy says. "Mr. Norris is a guy. Guys don't cry at books."

Jeremy has a lot of rules like this. Like not playing with girls at recess. Like not wearing pink socks, even if they're an accident. "Something must have run in the wash," I said so he knew I didn't *buy* them that way.

"Then you *throw them away*," he whispered.

I know he doesn't say these things to be mean. Jeremy is my best friend this year, I'm lucky to have him, I remind myself all the time. Still I sometimes wish he'd keep his helpful suggestions to himself.

I figured this out: Jeremy is nice to me about 75 percent of the time; 25 percent of the time he says things to remind me that he's better than me at everything. The other day he told me he was happy to be in this class, because he'd heard Mr.

Norris was such an easy grader. "I got mostly ones last year so I shouldn't worry, but still, it's nice to know."

Jeremy isn't like Lisa. He doesn't care if Mr. Norris is fun or inspiring. He cares about getting good grades.

"I'm glad I got him because I want to see him dress up like someone from Colonial times," I said.

Jeremy looked at me funny. "What are you talking about?"

"Haven't you heard about that? He picks a day and comes in dressed up like Benjamin Franklin or someone like that."

"That's not true."

"It is. I heard it from someone who had him five years ago."

"Well that was five years ago then. He hasn't done that since. That's what happens, Benny. Teachers have a lot of energy when they first start out and then they get tired. They can't keep it up and they burn out."

I thought about Mr. Norris falling asleep in class. Maybe Jeremy was right.

"Yeah, I'd say his best days are definitely behind him," Jeremy said. "You were the one who figured that out first."

No, I wasn't. "I was worried that something is wrong with him, not that he's a bad teacher."

Jeremy shrugged. "Same difference. All I can say is he

better not be a hard grader after this. I'll be really mad if he is."

That afternoon, it's raining so hard Mr. Norris tells us we'll have to stay inside for recess. I go to the book corner, where I see *Little House in the Big Woods.* I pull it out and start reading. A few minutes later, Mr. Norris comes over and stands next to me. "How do you like that one so far?" he says.

"It's good," I say, even though I've been reading the same sentence for a while because I haven't really been paying attention. Usually I read Garfield books at indoor recess. "I like reading about pioneer life."

"*Do* you?" he says, squinting his eyes.

"Actually, not really."

"So why were you reading it?"

"I have this friend, Lisa Lowes. She said I should read it."

"Hey, I remember that name."

Suddenly I feel embarrassed. Maybe I shouldn't have said anything, but I've been wanting to say her name all year so maybe Mr. Norris will notice me more.

"How is she doing?"

"Oh, pretty good."

"She was quite the firecracker back when I knew her. Tell

her I say hi." He makes a face standing up, like his knees hurt from crouching.

"I will," I say. "She really liked you. You were her favorite teacher of all time."

He looks down at me, surprised. "I *was*?" His eyebrows go up. "I'm not sure about that. I remember Lisa and me going head-to-head a little bit."

Sometimes Mr. Norris talks in ways that are hard to understand. Like what does it mean if he calls someone a firecracker? Does that mean she's full of sparks or does that mean she's someone who explodes when you don't want her to? And going head-to-head sounds like fighting, but how could they have fought if she loved him so much?

"I'll bet she's changed a lot," Mr. Norris says. "Lisa could be a little hard on some of her fellow students back when I knew her. But we talked about it and she worked on it. She got much better by the end of the year."

Wait, I think. Is he saying that Lisa was a *mean girl*? I can hardly believe it.

He shakes his head and keeps going. "She was particularly hard on a girl in our class who had Down syndrome. Usually I try not to interfere too much with peer dynamics, but I couldn't sit back in that case. I had to take a pretty strong stand. There were a few times I had to ask Lisa to leave the room."

I remember the way she cried when I told her I'd gotten Mr. Norris for my teacher. How she wished she could be in fourth grade again. This makes no sense.

"I'm sure she's changed a lot." He claps his hands. "Everyone grows up, right?"

NINE

I KEEP THINKING ABOUT MY LEGO MOVIES the whole time I'm still trying to do nice things and earn stupid footprints. I keep thinking of ideas where my Lego minifigs are in the same kind of contest. Where Batman's archenemies like Penguin and Joker and Riddler are competing to see who can do the most anonymous, nice things for one another. In my story, they spend all day making each other apple pies and cups of cappuccino.

I wonder if that would be funny. Maybe not so much.

Recently I got a better idea. After I told my mom Mr. Norris wasn't doing a lot of the things he'd done with Lisa's class, like dressing up and reading *The Indian in the Cupboard* out loud, she checked the book out of the library and brought it home. "You don't have to wait for Mr. Norris to read this to you," she said. In the past, she and Dad used to take turns reading books to us, even though we're all old enough to read books to ourselves. Usually they just read to me and George, but sometimes even Martin listens. Since Dad's accident though, no one's read to us at night. I hadn't even realized that until Mom started reading again and it felt like a sound that I hadn't heard in a long time.

I'll say this. Mom is pretty good at the different accents. The main character is an English boy who gets a plastic Indian for his birthday from his friend. From his older brother, he gets an old cupboard the brother found by the garbage in the alley. When he puts the Indian in the cupboard at night, he wakes up in the morning and the Indian is alive. It turns out he's not only alive, but he's a real person from history, an Iroquois who's fighting battles with the French and English. So Mom has to talk like him, which George loves because he doesn't talk very well. George keeps laughing until Mom tells him it isn't really funny. "In fact," she says, "it perpetuates a lot of negative stereotypes about Native Americans, which is probably why Mr. Norris isn't reading this book out loud to his class anymore."

Then she looks at my face and she knows what I'm

thinking: *I understand what you're saying, but I still like the part about toys coming to life and I want to hear the rest of it.*

She smiles at me and squeezes my hand. She keeps reading.

We're only halfway through the story, but the interesting part to me is how busy the boy gets taking care of his toys that have come to life. He has to keep them fed and warm and make places for them to sleep, along with the horses they were both riding that have also come alive. As if that's not hard enough, as the story goes along, he also has to worry about their feelings and helping them get along with each other.

Little Bear, the Indian, wants a wife and more tribesmen to help him fight the battle he was in the middle of back home, so Omri (that's the kid's name. I know—I don't get it either) has to worry about that, too. I don't know yet how it turns out, but all day at school, as I'm holding open doors and complimenting the cafeteria ladies on their tacos (which is the only food anyone can honestly compliment them on), I keep thinking I'd give anything for a magic cupboard that would bring my Lego minifigs to life. Then I could be really kind to them and earn a zillion footprints for that.

I have four favorite minifigs that I've carried around in

my pocket and played with so much their faces are almost worn off. Two are from Star Wars sets—Senator Palpatine and Count Dooku—and two from Batman—the Riddler and Penguin. Mom once asked me why all my favorite minifigs are the bad guys, and I explained it's because they're strong and they're also the people who need friends the most. If my Batman minifig came to life the same size he is now—that's what happens in the book, the plastic people stay small—would he need a big kid to help him out? My guess is, honestly, probably not.

Also, if Batman came to life, he wouldn't want me to make him food or build him a house—he'd want Alfred, his butler, to do all that stuff. I'd bring Alfred to life and while I was at it, Robin, too, and then my work would pretty much be done.

With the Riddler and Penguin it wouldn't be that way. We'd have to work together since they have no other friends and no one else likes them. Maybe this is how Omri feels in the book when he brings Little Bear to life. In every movie Omri's seen, the Indian is the bad guy (I'm pretty sure he lived before the Batman and Star Wars movies), but even if the guy is shooting arrows and swinging a hatchet, how bad could he be if he's small enough to stand in the palm of your hand? The answer is: not that bad.

That's how I feel about my guys. I get to know them better and I like them more. I always think bad guys make better movies. Look at *Pirates of the Caribbean*.

Ever since that conversation with Olga about spending lunch periods working on her comic books in the library, I've been thinking about asking Mr. Norris if I could do the same thing, only I'd go to the computer lab, where they have movie-editing software that I learned how to use once, but I've never been able to try it again because my class always has an assignment during computer lab time.

"You're thinking about doing *what*?" Jeremy says at lunchtime. Rayshawn is eating at another table today. He goes back and forth between two tables and, I can't help it, I always feel a little sad when he doesn't sit with Jeremy and me. Maybe because I like the way he laughs and shakes his head and says "sheesh" at the things Jeremy sometimes says.

"Going to the computer lab. To ask if I could edit something there."

"Edit *what*?" Jeremy stares at me.

"Just something I'm working on."

"Like what? Tell me."

I'm not sure why I started all this. "Just these little movies I make. It's not that big a deal. I don't play anything at recess anyway."

It's true—the last few days Rayshawn has asked me to play basketball with two of his friends who are fifth graders. I'm pretty sure he's kidding because the other guys are really good and so is he, so I haven't played with them but I've stood on the sidelines and watched. They were so good, I wondered if Rayshawn asked me out of pity as a way to get a footprint.

That would definitely be the worst way to get my name on a footprint—where I'm someone else's good deed. *No thanks,* I decided last week, and stayed away from basketball. Now I have to admit Olga's idea of skipping recess completely sounds pretty good. The problem is Mr. Norris already said no. "She's got a medical excuse, Benny. Even so, all kids need to get exercise and Olga gets hers walking a lap around the building before school starts."

Couldn't I do that? I wanted to say, but part of me feels like I already walk down enough hallways with Olga and I don't need any more reasons for people to think we're best friends.

As I walked away from Mr. Norris's desk, he must have

felt sorry for me, because he said, "We couldn't make it a regular thing, Benny, but if you'd like me to write you the *occasional* pass to go to the computer lab for recess, I will."

I smiled. He smiled back.

"But let's wait for the days when you *really* need it, okay?" he said.

That reminded me of something my (old) dad would have said. In fact, he did say it a few times when he was coaching soccer and I was pretending to have a hurt ankle. "I'll let you sit out a quarter, Benny, but how about if we wait for the games when you *really* need that?"

He meant the games where the kids on the other side were really big and scary good. We played a few games like that, where the other team seemed like they'd gotten lost on the way to a high school game. We'd sit on our side and watch them warm up: one kid would head butt the ball to another kid, who'd catch it with his ankle. Sometimes even then, I'd feel bad about asking my dad to sit out—like maybe next week the other team would be even scarier.

That's what's happened with the recess pass. I haven't asked for one because I haven't thought I *really* needed it.

Jeremy stops asking about my movies pretty quickly. That's one good thing about Jeremy. If you don't want to talk about something, he's not so curious that he'll keep asking questions.

That day at recess I spend most of the time sitting near the basketball court, planning the new movie I've gotten an idea for. It's partly based on *The Indian in the Cupboard* only it'll be the reverse. We'll see the characters first as real people in their real movies and then they'll wake up as plastic minifigs. If I download scenes from their original movies, it could be really great. Like we could see Count Dooku in the middle of a laser sword fight and then suddenly he wakes up, little and plastic. Then he runs into some other minifigs from other movies and the same thing has happened to them.

They'll all start asking one another, "How did this happen? How did we get so small and so plastic?"

Then they'll go to Lego Yoda, who'll explain, "Popularity and success, this means. Plastic, it makes you. Fight back your way to your old story."

I have to stop there because the recess bell rings and Rayshawn is standing next to me, looking down at my pages. "Whatcha got there?" he says, wiping his upper lip with the back of his hand.

"A plot outline for a Lego movie," I tell him. I have no

idea why I can say this so easily to Rayshawn when I have never told Jeremy.

"For real?" Rayshawn says, crouching to study my quick drawings.

"It's just something I play around with. It's not a big deal," I say.

"But you know how to make a movie? You have a movie camera and all that?"

I want to say, *Everyone does, Rayshawn, just open your parents' phone.* But the truth is I *do* have a decent camera. Last year, when Dad saw that I was serious about making movies, he brought out an old movie camera he used when we were little and showed me how to set it up on a tripod.

"And you can make it look like those guys are moving around? Like having fights and stuff?"

"Oh yeah, the fights are easy. Dialogue is a little harder. You have to dub that in afterward."

He tells me he likes my drawings and lifts the corner of one page so he can look at the next one. I'm not a bad artist.

As we're walking inside, he asks me more questions: How do I get the guys to move without showing my fingers? Doesn't it take forever, one frame at a time? After I've explained everything, I almost ask him if he wants to come over and help me make a movie this weekend, but then I remember what happened when Lisa came over. I picture my dad hugging Rayshawn. I would die, I think. I would really die.

I start the movie by myself over the weekend. I shoot the first scene, where each character wakes up and realizes their stubby plastic arms only bend at the shoulder and their legs have no knees. I have to say it's pretty good. Since I don't have a friend to help me, I get George, who turns out to be fine at pressing the shutter release when I say "Go!" which is great. It means I don't have to get up every two seconds. When I made movies with Kenneth, I gave him this job, but he always thought I was moving the guys too much between each shot, so we had to waste a lot of time arguing about that. George doesn't even look at the shot. He just likes the sound the camera makes when he presses the button, so he stays with it for a surprisingly long time and it goes faster than I've ever shot a scene before. In the last scene we shoot, I have all my main characters stand in a square (no circles in Lego world!) and try to decide what to do.

"What do you think should happen now?" I ask George over lunch.

He rocks a little. "Don't know!" he says into his hand.

"Is George really helping you?" Mom asks, surprised.

"Yeah. He's a good cameraman actually. Better than Kenneth was."

Mom puts some more mac and cheese on my plate and kisses the top of my head. "That's because you're a great teacher, Benny. You're probably the best teacher George has. Don't tell Martin I said that."

I think Mom says things like this because it's not always easy hanging out with George and being his teacher. Like in the afternoon when we go back to shoot some more, he doesn't want to listen to me. He just wants to keep pressing the shutter and hearing the sound until finally I have to get so mad at him Mom comes into the room and says we're both going to lose all of our screen time if we don't stop fighting.

So that's what a great teacher for George I am. Earlier, when Mom said that, I thought, *Maybe she'll tell Mr. Norris and he'll write that on a footprint.* It's like even though I'm pretending to care less these days, it's still this big stupid thing I keep thinking about.

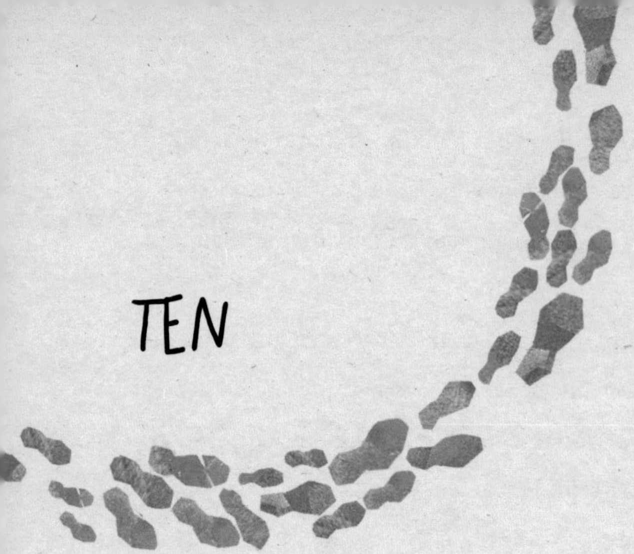

TEN

ON MONDAY SOMETHING REALLY SURPRISING happens. At lunch, Ms. Crocker comes over to the table where Jeremy and I are sitting and sits down next to us. "Oh, Benny, I just heard about what happened to your dad this summer. I'm so sorry. Is he doing better now?"

At first I'm so embarrassed I don't know what to say. I haven't told Jeremy anything about what happened to my dad. Every time I think about it, I picture Lisa screaming *"Get him off of me!"* Or I remember Jeremy asking if George was an alien contacting his mother ship, like he seriously thought that was a possibility. What will he say if I tell him my dad has no hair, a scary scar, and forgets almost everything you tell him these days?

I feel my face burn red, but I know I have to say something. "He's okay," I say. "It takes a while I guess, but he's a lot better than he was."

"Good."

I'm blushing like this is a lie, even though it's not. These days, he does seem better about half the time. Like in the morning he'll come down while we're eating breakfast and say hi to everyone. Sometimes he'll look a little surprised, like he forgot how many kids he had, or how big we've gotten, but he usually he seems happy. The afternoons are harder. A lot of times he's asleep when we get home. If he gets woken up, he's usually in a terrible mood. He'll tell us we have to go outside even if we're not making that much noise. Sometimes it's only George humming, but even that is too much. He'll say his head is about to explode if someone doesn't turn off whatever's making that noise.

"You let us know if there's anything your family needs," Ms. Crocker says. "That's what we're here for, Benny."

I try to think of something I could ask her for. Should I tell her, *My mom seems pretty worried about money? If the school wanted to give us some, that would be great.*

Obviously I'm not going to say that. I have enough things to be embarrassed about.

Jeremy waits until after Ms. Crocker walks away to ask, "What happened to your dad?"

"He had an operation this summer on his brain."

"Oh." Jeremy nods. "Is he okay?"

"Yeah. I mean, sort of. It takes a while for the brain to get completely back to normal, I guess. So he still can't do certain things." I feel like I can't lie to him completely. But I'm also not going to tell him that this morning my dad couldn't remember the word for oatmeal. "Mostly he's okay."

He narrows his eyes in a way that makes me nervous. Like he's trying to decide if all this is too much and he shouldn't be my friend: first my brother, now my dad.

I wait forever until he finally says, "I think Ms. Crocker's going to give you a footprint."

This isn't what I expected him to say, but I have to admit, I like the idea. It would be one thing to get a footprint from Mr. Norris after all these days of trying and waiting. It would be something else completely to get one from Ms. Crocker. "What do you mean? What for?"

"Because she feels sorry for you." I can tell it makes him mad. "That's the whole point of footprints, right? It's about doing nice things for people you feel sorry for."

No, I want to say. *That's not the whole idea.* Instead I shake my head. "I doubt it. What does my dad's surgery have to do with getting a footprint?"

Jeremy turns and looks at me. "Exactly," he says.

That afternoon Mr. Norris starts reading a new book because he finished *So B. It* (which never says the mom is autistic, but she definitely is). This time it's a book called *Zen Shorts,* but here's the weird part—it's a picture book! In fourth grade!

"This footprints program has gotten a lot of us thinking about kindness, hasn't it?" Mr. Norris says. "I know a lot of you are trying to think of ways to show kindness to one another, so I thought maybe it would help if I read some stories about that."

Yes! I think. *It would help a lot!*

Then he reads one of the stories. It's about a man who wakes up to find a burglar in his house, stealing all his things. Instead of getting mad at the burglar, the man looks down at the bathrobe he's wearing. It's the only thing the burglar hasn't taken. "Would you like this?" he says, offering the bathrobe. When the robber asks why he's giving him everything, the man says, "I'm not. I still have the moon."

Everyone laughs at that one. Ha! The moon! Yeah right!

But I think most of us get the main point—we shouldn't be too greedy about toys or clothes. The problem is, it's not like any of us know any burglars to give our bathrobes to. If we did though, it's a pretty safe bet that all of us would.

ELEVEN

THE NEXT DAY, I CAN'T HELP it. I walk straight up the hallway where the line of footprints has stretched almost to the art room and look for my name on the new footprints that have been put up on the wall. All night I kept thinking about what Jeremy said: that Ms. Crocker was going to give me a footprint because she feels sorry for me. I have to admit, it's raised my hopes. I keep thinking he's right. Ms. Crocker said, *"You let us know if there's anything your family needs."* Well, one thing she could do for our family would be to write up a bunch of footprints with my name on them!

I read over all the new footprints slowly, just to make sure I'm not missing any. Olga has one for helping the librarians put chairs away during lunchtime. Peter and James got one for "Finding a peaceful solution to their conflict." And then there's this, at the very end: *Jeremy Johnson helped Ms. Watusi, a new teacher, find paper for the copy machine.*

Jeremy's smiling big when I walk into class, like I should find this funny.

"Can you believe it?" he says. "What did that take me, like two seconds? I was waiting at the water fountain and she looked out of the supply closet and said, 'Does anyone know where the copy paper is?' I said, 'On the shelves underneath, I think.' Then she came out a minute later and asked me my name. Just as easy as that."

He laughs like all of this is a pretty funny joke.

I guess maybe it is unless the one thing you've learned in fourth grade is that you're bad at everything that comes easily to other people, and then it isn't so funny.

That afternoon George has a footprint, too. *George B. sat through chorus concert very nicely,* it says. I sat through the chorus concert very nicely, too. Afterward I told Hannah I liked her solo even though I couldn't hear it. No one could. She sang so softly, she looked like she was lip-synching and someone forgot to turn the CD player on. I still told her she was great, but guess how many footprints I got for that? Zero.

By Wednesday, there are footprints on the wall stretching from the front door around to the art room and first grade classrooms. There are too many footprints to count. Someone gets creative and puts some on the ceiling, which means I get dizzy trying to read those.

Some people already have two footprints. Four people have three footprints.

I still have no footprints. Even though I love Ms. Crocker and work hard every day at showing my compassion, empathy, and respect, I have no footprints. None at all.

"Maybe you should tell Mr. Norris," Jeremy says on Thursday afternoon. His face is serious. "I'm pretty sure everyone's supposed to have at least one by now."

On Friday I ask Mr. Norris if I'm doing something wrong to go so long without getting any footprints at all. He says no, it doesn't work that way. "They're meant to be a surprise for doing nice things *when you think no one is looking*." He whispers the last part.

"But no one is ever looking at me. Some people get

looked at and some people don't!"

Mr. Norris puts a hand on my back. I feel happy for the hand and sorry that I'm sitting here, almost crying in front of him. "The footprints shouldn't make anyone feel bad. I'll tell you a little secret, Benny. I think some teachers give footprints to the kids who have the hardest time figuring out what doing nice things for other people feels like. It doesn't come naturally to some kids. It comes so naturally to you that people forget to tell you because you're doing little nice things all the time."

I peek up at him. "I am?"

"Oh sure. I see it. You're a very nice friend to Jeremy. You don't complain when Gabriel kicks your feet in music class. You gave Rachel some of your lunch when she left hers at home."

I can hardly believe it! He's right! I've done *lots* of nice things! My footprints could get us all the way to the cafetorium if someone would just write them down!

"Here's the thing though, Benny. You know in your heart that you're one of the nicest kids I can think of. You shouldn't need footprints on a hall wall to prove that to yourself."

But I do! I want to scream. *Why shouldn't I need that! Plus the pizza party, too! "It's not fair, Mr. Norris,"* I want to scream and then I feel embarrassed because I realize that I have screamed it.

At home that afternoon, I lie down with Lucky. I think maybe I'll cry into her side for a little bit and then just lying there makes me feel so much better, I don't need to. That's the nice thing about Lucky. She doesn't know what happened to me today, she's just happy to have me on the dog bed with her. That's what's great about dogs.

TWELVE

FOR THREE DAYS I KEEP CHECKING the hall wall. Even though Mr. Norris never said he would write up the nice things he said about me, I keep expecting to see my name with the good deeds he mentioned. *Maybe there will be three footprints,* I think. *But two will be fine, or even one.* Then I can't believe it. There's nothing the next day. Or the day after that.

Four days later: still nothing.

Didn't he almost *promise* he'd write one? Wasn't the whole point of our talk that he saw me doing three nice things and felt bad because he hadn't written them down? Then I remember the last thing he said: *You shouldn't need footprints to prove that to yourself.*

Why would he say something like that?

On Friday, Jeremy gets another one hundred on the spelling test. I miss five words out of ten and get *See me* written on the bottom of my page.

When I go to talk to Mr. Norris, he doesn't even look up when he asks me if everything is all right at home. He's shuffling papers and looking in his drawers. *Maybe he's going to give me a lemon drop,* I think and then I remember that nothing else Lisa told me to expect has turned out to be true so why should that one be any different?

I'm right. He doesn't give me a lemon drop.

He shuts the drawer and looks at me. "I wanted to ask about your dad and how he's doing, Benny. I'm sorry I haven't done that yet. I'm still getting to know all of you and I wasn't sure if you wanted to talk about it or not."

"No," I say, though it's hard to tell what I'm answering because he hasn't asked a question. "I mean, it's okay. He's better now."

I try to imagine the teacher meeting where my name must have come up. I picture all the teachers hearing *brain surgery* and shaking their heads. Part of me wants everyone to feel sorry for us and part of me really *doesn't* want that. "The doctors say he's going to be totally fine. It'll just take some time."

No doctor has said this—at least not that I've heard—but Mom says it. I try to believe it. Maybe that's enough for Mr. Norris to believe it, too. "Maybe the question I should ask is, are *you* okay?"

"I guess so," I say softly. Mr. Norris has to lean closer to hear me.

"I know when parents get busy with other problems, sometimes the kid with the fewest problems might feel a little forgotten."

I feel like saying, *Are you kidding? You think I have no problems? Haven't you noticed all the orange slips with my name on them?* Whatever happens, though, I don't want to start crying right here in front of Mr. Norris and everyone else. I used to have a little problem with crying in school, especially in first grade, when everyone was obsessed with playing Uno and I always lost. Once I lost eight games in a row and no matter how much I told myself not to cry, I still did. I couldn't help it. In second grade, I learned a few different tricks to cover it up. I'd say I have allergies and sneeze a lot into a paper towel. Or I'd go to the nurse who, no matter what your problem is, always says, "Why don't you lie down for a few minutes and see if you don't feel better?"

Now that I've remembered this trick, I really need to use

it. I tell Mr. Norris I have a bad stomachache and he gives me a pass to the nurse's office. Usually it's a relief to go to the nurse's office, where she keeps the lie-down room dark, so it's fine to cry in there without too many people figuring out what you're doing, but today I walk in and find someone is already there. Even worse: it's George, lying in the dark, flicking a pencil over his face back and forth, and singing the "Garden Song." He doesn't look in the least bit sick. I have no idea what he's doing in here.

He doesn't look at me when I walk in. He just keeps singing: "'Inch by inch, row by row. Gonna make my garden grow . . .'"

"You can't sing in here, George," I say. "You have to be quiet. This room is supposed to be for sick people."

He ignores me the way he always ignores people when he feels like it and keeps singing.

"We don't mind," the nurse calls from the other room. "George likes the echo in there. He comes here to sing when he's finished his work."

George gets weird rewards for doing things that other kids are just expected to do, like finishing his work. Usually his reward is visiting the custodian's office to look at the floor waxer. George has never seen the floor waxer plugged in because it only gets used at night when no kids are here, but still it's his favorite machine of all time. At the end of my first day of kindergarten, George was allowed to take me from class and walk me down the hall to see the floor waxer. I'd heard about it for years, and I had to admit, it was very big and pretty cool.

"So if you're done with your work, why aren't you visiting the floor waxer?" I ask now.

"Don't know!" he says and laughs. Maybe he doesn't love it so much anymore. Maybe he's changing, like Mr. Norris, only I didn't even realize it.

I lie down on the cot next to him. Instead of asking what I'm doing there, he looks over at me and starts singing the song he always sings around me, "Benny and the Jets." It's by a guy named Elton John, who used to dress crazy but doesn't anymore. "'He's got electric boots! A mohair suit! You know I read it in a maga-zine! Benny and the Jets!'"

George doesn't know what the song is about. Mom says no one does, probably.

It's George's way of saying hello. He doesn't do anything like other people. He doesn't say *Hi* or *Are you sick?* or *What are you doing in the nurse's office?* He just switches the song that he's singing way too loud.

George can be a really good singer sometimes. Other times, his singing sounds awful.

Mom says it's because George likes playing games with his voice. That sometimes "disconsonant singing" is more interesting to his ears than singing a song perfectly in tune. I don't know what "disconsonant" means but I assume it means "bad sounding."

I came here because I wanted to cry for a few minutes about my test and now I have to sit in the lie-down room with George singing too loud. "Could you stop singing, George? *Please?*"

He doesn't stop. He never does unless someone threatens to take away his screen time if he doesn't stop. For the rest of us, it means losing TV and video games. For George, it means he can't watch the stupid YouTube videos he loves of people falling down and cats doing crazy things like climbing curtains. The rest of us wouldn't care, but George cares a lot about dumb cat videos.

Finally I wait for a pause in the song and say, "If you don't stop, I'll tell Mom to take away your screen."

He stops and I cry for a little bit. I know I'm too old to care as much as I do about spelling tests or footprints. I also know that I'm not really crying about these. I'm crying because this morning Mom told me she's taking Dad in for a doctor's appointment where they'll do tests to measure how well his brain is recovering. According to Mom, the tests are full of strange questions and it's hard to predict how he'll do. A question on one of the other tests was: *If I were a fire, what color would I be?* Dad looked at the woman, confused, like he wanted to say, *You're not a fire.*

I guess weird phrasing is the point of these questions. Mom says they're testing his *abstract* thinking, which is different from *concrete* thinking. He has to be able to imagine certain things and then answer questions based on what he's imagining. "For example, George can't do much abstract thinking," she said this morning to explain. All that did was make me more nervous—like at the end of all this, Dad is going to come out like George.

This morning when Mom reminded Dad that he had his big test today, he started to groan like George does when he has to turn off the TV. He acted like a child, which was terrible to see. I know everyone says what happened to Dad wasn't my fault, but if it wasn't my fault, then whose fault was it? It was *my* helmet hitting his head, *my* stupid clumsiness making us crash in the first place. If I was a different person—or a better bike rider, at least—I wouldn't have flown off my bike into Dad. He wouldn't have bumped his head hard enough for it to bleed into itself. I wouldn't be lying here crying and wondering how his test is going today when mine went so badly.

THIRTEEN

AT HOME THAT AFTERNOON, I CAN'T concentrate enough to do my homework so I go up to my room and lie down on my bed. Mom and Dad still aren't back from the doctor and I can't help it. I feel like crying again. Martin comes into my room with an old carton of ice cream. It's a boring flavor—vanilla—so no one has eaten it for a while and there's an icy crust on top. I know because I looked at it earlier and decided not to eat it.

"Heard you had a tough day," he says, handing me the carton and an extra spoon. He's eaten through the worst parts. It's not too bad. I'm surprised he knows about my day, but I guess George's ramblings say more than I think. Martin must have listened for a while and figured out that I was crying in the nurse's office. "So what happened?"

I shrug. I don't feel like going into all the details. "I just feel so stupid. Why can't I be a better bike rider?"

He sits down on my bed next to my feet. "I'll tell you something. I know it seems like a big deal now, but by the time you get to middle school no one cares much about bike riding."

He's probably right. I can't remember the last time I saw Martin riding his bike.

"There's a lot of things that seem super important when you're a kid and then it turns out, guess what, they don't really matter when you're grown-up."

Is he saying he's a grown-up now? I can't tell. "Most grown-ups can ride a bike," I say.

"Yeah, but you know what? If they can't, who's gonna know? Don't get on one and don't advertise the fact, right? Get good at other things. No one's standing there with a checklist at middle school."

I have to admit, it's nice to hear him say this. We eat for a while, passing the carton back and forth, until it's empty.

"So what's happening with Lisa?" I finally ask.

I know they're still going out, but she hasn't been over to the house since that day when Dad hugged her too long, and

Martin hasn't talked about her too much. "I don't know," he says, shaking his head. "It's weird. I'm not sure if I really like Lisa that much anymore."

I'm surprised. "But isn't she still your girlfriend?"

"Right. I mean that's the problem. I know everyone says I'm so lucky, she's so great and all that, but—"

I stare at him. "But *what*?"

He throws away the carton. "Okay, here's the problem. Do you remember that girl, Mary Margaret, who I was partners with for sixth grade science fair?"

I do, but barely. I was in first grade and visited their booth with the rest of my class. I didn't understand how she could have *two* names. I still don't, actually.

"So we've always been friends since then. Real friends. Like, she was the first girl I could laugh with. We've always had these inside jokes and she makes fun of me and whatever. We text a lot over the weekend, even though we don't really do anything or hang out, right?"

I didn't know any of this.

"So this whole thing with Lisa—we've been going out for, what? Six months?"

"Seven," I correct him. "You started last March."

"Right. Seven. So it's been a while. We should know each other pretty well by now, but we still have these times where we'll be sitting at lunch and she'll be telling some story and I'll think—oh my God, I stopped listening to her like twenty minutes ago. I can't help it. Most of the time I have no idea what she's talking about. It usually has to do with all her friends and who's in a fight with who and I just don't care. And the thing is, she does the *exact same thing* to me. I'll be talking about something that happened with my friends and I can tell she's not listening even though it's a hilarious story, and I'll get to the end and she'll say, 'Are you really still friends with those guys, 'cause you should think about that.'"

"Did she really say that?"

He nods. "She has this idea that she can make me part of the popular crowd if she just works hard enough at it. Lately I keep thinking, I'm not sure I even *like* Lisa's crowd. And then I keep thinking, I have a way easier time talking to Mary Margaret than I do to Lisa."

I can't believe what he's saying. Part of me feels like I'll kill him if he breaks up with Lisa, who I still love because she paid so much attention to me over the summer. And then I remember what Mr. Norris almost said and then didn't quite.

Maybe Lisa isn't a very nice girl.

Martin's old friends don't play sports or date popular girls. Some of them are pretty geeky, but if you get to know them, they're all funny and they're all pretty nice. Not that any of them have been over since Dad's accident but that's not their fault. Like I said, no one has, except for Lisa, which made us too scared to try it again.

Martin once told me he had a test for new friends. He invited them to our house and didn't say anything ahead of time about George. If they were decently nice when George bounced in, flapping his hands and talking to himself, he knew they were okay. Then he would tell them, "Yeah, he's autistic," like it wasn't *that* weird a thing. Mostly they'd nod and say "cool," and keep doing whatever they were doing, which was usually playing a video game.

I don't know why we can't do the same thing with Dad, but for some reason we just can't. Autism is a thing other kids recognize; Dad's problems aren't.

"So do you like Mary Margaret now?" I ask. I still can't get over this weird two-name thing; I also can't really remember what she looks like except she has brown hair and I'm pretty sure she wears glasses.

Martin smiles and shakes his head. "I know this sounds crazy but I kind of *do*."

I don't get it. "Why is that crazy?"

"We've been friends for so long that it's a little weird. I can't figure out if I *really* like her or if I like her because she's the opposite of Lisa."

I don't have any advice on this. I can't help it though, I start to feel sorry for Lisa. Part of me still loves her a little bit. I think about Lisa saying I was a great little brother. When someone is pretty like Lisa, it's confusing.

When they finally get home, Mom tells us the tests mostly went okay. Dad couldn't do everything they asked, but when he had trouble remembering a list of unrelated words (*blanket, rabbit, barrette*) he made a joke instead of getting frustrated.

I smile as she tells the story. I'm pretty relieved. "What was the joke?"

"He said, 'Blanket, some small animal, hair thing.'" She laughs at it, remembering. "I don't know. I thought it was funny."

It is *funny,* I think. Maybe he *will* be okay. Maybe we'll get through this because we've lived with George twelve years and we know how to laugh at people saying strange things that aren't really funny.

FOURTEEN

THE PROBLEM WITH HAVING A GREAT setup for a Lego movie is that you can't keep having characters repeat what they've already said. They can't keep looking down at their feet and saying, "Holy mackerel—I'm Lego!" Even if it makes a super funny scene, which it does.

They have to *do* something.

That's the secret of moviemaking, I've learned. People have to do something and then, at the end of the scene, they need to have another scene and do something else. I have two great scenes finished so far. In one, the four main characters realize they're stuck, and in another Yoda tells them, in his Yoda way, that it happened because their movies are so successful.

But what can they *do* to get back into the movies they came from? Should there be a magic spell? Should there be a surprising Lego minifig who has lots of power even though in his movie, he has none? Someone like Chewbacca, who's just a Bigfoot joke in the movie, but maybe in Lego world he's like the Wizard of Oz, the guy who everyone looks up to, even if he can't exactly grant their wishes.

I've seen *The Lego Movie* a few times and it doesn't really help for what I'm trying to do here. That one didn't use the same minifigs that I love. What I'm doing is more like *The Indian in the Cupboard*, but Mom has been reading more of that story and it's going in a different direction than I expected. Now it's all about Omri's family and his friend Patrick. I don't want to make this story about myself or anyone else in the family.

Which means I have to figure out how these minifigs can solve their own problems.

It's been a week since Martin and I had our talk in my room about life and bike riding and Lisa and I keep thinking about him saying he might like Mary Margaret more than Lisa, even though she isn't as glamorous or as pretty. He liked talking to her more, he'd said.

It's made me notice something. I sort of like talkin[g to] Olga.

Not *that way* of course. Please. I'm in fourth grade, give me a break.

But Olga's nice. And a lot of the things she says make sense. I've figured this much out: she's not bad at math or spelling. Her main problem is that her eyes don't work together right so lines of print slide around on the page for her. It turns out she's pretty smart, though. She's much better than I am at remembering the stories we're reading. She's also fine with her multiplication tables—she just can't write the answers in the right order on the page, so she does horrible on the tests, but she knows all the facts. We've even developed this system where she helps me out by putting her fingers on her knees. I think she's been doing it for a while, but I didn't catch on until last week. I was trying to do 3 times 7—counting in my head, trying to add 14 plus 7—but the numbers kept getting mixed up and then I looked over and saw her holding two fingers on one knee and one finger on the other.

"Twenty-one?" I said.

Ms. LeNice, our math tutor, smiled. "Very good, Benny!"

Ms. LeNice hasn't figured out our system, so we still do it, but here's the funny part. Every time we get away with one of our cheats, I remember that math fact afterward: 3 times 7? Twenty-one. No problem. So maybe this is just another learning technique.

It's ended up making Olga and me better friends, which makes me wish the other girls were nicer to her. She says she doesn't care about the other girls. "I have *friends.* Just not the other girls in our class. We don't have enough in common."

I wonder if she's got a point with this. I think about Jeremy and what we have in common. Not too much is the truth. Mostly what we have in common is that we both needed a friend this year. Me because Kenneth moved away. Him because he's never had one. Not a real one, anyway. When I went over to his house a few weeks ago, he said, "You're the first friend who's come over here in a long time," which was a sad thing to say, but Jeremy didn't seem to think so.

We didn't do too much. Mostly I watched him play computer games I don't know. It wasn't all that much fun.

That's why I understand what Martin's saying about Lisa. He feels like he's supposed to like her because he got lucky and she decided to like him. The problem is—he just doesn't. He doesn't think she's that much fun and he doesn't act like himself around her. What's to like?

This is how I feel with Jeremy and all his rules. I shouldn't talk about Lego and I shouldn't talk to girls and I shouldn't wear slightly pink socks. I end up never saying much of anything. Mostly I nod and eat my lunch. What's to like?

With Olga, it's different. Because she told me about her comic books, I surprise myself and tell her about my Lego movie just like I told Rayshawn. At first I make it like a question, about how I can get permission to use the school's movie-editing software. Ms. Bukowski, the computer teacher, isn't very friendly and I can't imagine asking her.

"No, don't ask her," Olga tells me. "She says no to everyone. You have to make friends with Ms. Johnson, the librarian, and show her you're pretty serious about your project. Like spend a few lunch periods there and bring in the work you've done at home. Then she'll talk to Ms. Bukowski about letting you use the computers. That's what I did."

I think about this. I can't very well bring my camera, tripod, and Lego guys in. Lunch would be over by the time I'd set everything up. But I could bring in my plans and spend lunch period figuring out what should happen next.

At home that afternoon, I finish my homework quickly and I'm setting up my Lego guys so I can film a little more when Dad comes in. At first I think maybe he wants to help, which would be great. Maybe he can do the same thing George was doing before we started fighting and he refused to help me anymore.

"Do you want to be my cameraman, Dad?" I say.

He looks surprised so I point to the camera to remind him what I'm talking about. "Oh my!" he says, touching it. "That looks interesting." He remembers enough to get behind it and look at the screen. I've zoomed it in on Count Dooku holding up a light saber. I want to film a short scene where he's practice fighting by himself.

"You just press the shutter when I say go. . . ."

He doesn't remember where the shutter button is so I point it out. "Oh, right here," he says. "Sure."

We take a few shots and then he asks if I have a chair he can sit down in. I should remember this is his main problem—he gets tired so easily. After he sits, he does great though. He presses the shutter every time I say go and pretty soon I've finished the scene. We high-five and laugh. It feels like the old Dad is coming back more and more.

"You know what I think we should do?" he says, standing up and pulling me into a one-arm hug. This is the first time since the accident that he's suggested something. At least it's the first time that I've heard him do it.

I fall against him, happy. "What?" *Dad is back,* I think. *He's going to be okay.*

"I think you should ride your bike at the track while I run my laps."

I freeze on the spot. I pull away. His face is blank, like he has no idea what he's just said. *"Dad,"* I say. "I don't want to do that."

He looks confused. "Why not?"

"That's how you got—"

I look at his face. He doesn't remember anything. If Mom has gone over it—which I'm sure she has—he doesn't remember that either.

"Not right now, Dad," I say. "I have a lot of homework."

"All right." He smiles and nods. "Maybe tomorrow."

FIFTEEN

HERE'S THE WEIRDEST PART: DAD WILL say something like that at night and the next day he'll seem really, truly better. In the morning he's in a great mood, asking everyone about their day ahead. When we get home from school, he's in the kitchen fixing us all a snack. After we eat, George gets on the computer to watch YouTube videos, which he's allowed to do if he's earned sixteen stars at school. Even though it's October and way too early for Christmas, he types in *Santa Claus* and watches videos of people dressed up as Santa doing dumb things. George loves Santa and everything Christmas related and could watch these videos all day long. Usually our parents make him wait until after Halloween before he's allowed to start obsessing over Christmas, but this year those old rules don't apply so much, I guess.

Dad stands behind George, watching the videos, laughing along with the jokes. He's leaning against his cane, but otherwise he looks more like his old self than he has in a while. If this was two months ago, Mom would probably say, "Oh, Brian, don't encourage him." With her friends, she sometimes said, "I feel like I have four boys." Since his accident, she never makes that joke of course. But now Dad looks so normal, she almost could. George laughs at the video of Santa sneezing on some sugar, then Dad laughs, too. It's so great to see, I laugh along. Dad turns and sees me. "Hey, Benny, there you are! I wanted to ask you something."

"What?"

"What about bringing your bike to the track? You know, the one at the high school?"

Why won't he let this go? It's like his brain is caught in the loop of what he was thinking right before it broke. "I don't think so, Dad," I say.

"Why not?" He makes a sad face. "You need to push yourself a little, Benny. Don't be afraid. I wasted too much time as a kid being scared of sports."

No, Dad, I want to say. *You weren't scared enough.*

When Mom comes back in the room, I don't say anything. She asks George and me to take Lucky for a walk before dinner. Usually I would tell her it's Martin's turn because I'm pretty sure it is, but today I don't mind getting away from Dad, who can't stop obsessing over this bike-riding thing.

One of the few things that hasn't changed since Dad's accident is the program Mom started last year where we're all supposed to do six chores a week to get our allowance but we get credit if we help George do a chore. When I tell him what we're doing, George gets off the computer and finds Lucky's leash.

Once we get outside, I can't stop thinking about this weird obsession everyone has with my bike riding. I ask George how he got so good at bike riding. He doesn't answer, of course. George almost never answers a question like this. I know he heard it, though, because he says "Bike riding!" and jogs a little ahead of me.

Walking with George isn't like walking with other people. You don't walk side by side and you don't really talk to each other. When George is outside, he likes saying lines from whatever he's been watching lately. If you ask him what it's from, he always acts surprised, like he can't believe you just heard what he's thinking. I don't think he realizes how much he says out loud.

After two blocks, I put my hand on George's elbow because there's someone up ahead with a dog. I warn him because sometimes, when another dog is around, George will get scared and drop Lucky's leash. "Look," I say and point. "Dog ahead."

As we walk closer, I hear George say, "Lisa Lowes!" into his hand and I realize he's right: it *is* Lisa Lowes walking toward us.

It's too late to pretend we haven't seen her. "Benny!" She smiles like she's happy to see me. Her dog pulls her over to sniff Lucky. "I miss you! I feel like I haven't seen you in forever!"

I blush because I know exactly how long it's been: four weeks. "We miss you, too," I say. I have to be careful and remember to say "we."

She looks at George, who has bounced away from us and onto someone's lawn so he doesn't have to say anything. "Do you think George remembers me?"

I can't believe she's asking this because of course he remembers her. He's only walking away because she makes him nervous. "Oh sure. Don't you remember how he cleared your plate the last time you ate at our house?"

She gives me a strange look like, *What are you talking about?*

Then she looks at George, pacing on someone's lawn, talking into his hand, which he sometimes does. "He should probably get off of there, right?"

She doesn't say it very nicely. Unfortunately, she's probably right but there's a zillion things George shouldn't do and he does them anyway. Walking on other people's lawns isn't the worst of it. I'm sorry, it just isn't.

Still, she looks at me like I should do something.

I shrug. "Somebody will say something if they mind. Mostly people don't mind."

She turns away, shaking her head, like something else is wrong.

"Lisa? Are you okay?"

"Did Martin tell you that he and I got in a fight today?"

"No."

"He thinks we need to give each other space." For a second I thought she was crying but now I see that she's definitely not. She's too mad. Her lips are folded and her arms are crossed. She looks a little bit like Poison Ivy from *Batman*, planning her revenge. "He's such a jerk. He really is. He's not going to have a lot of friends after this."

I'm not going to tell her that I'm pretty sure Martin's friends don't care too much about her one way or the other.

"I'm talking about friends *that matter,*" she says, almost as if she heard what I was thinking. "Not those stupid old friends of his. Those guys are losers. He should have listened to me when I told him to stop hanging out with them."

I can't believe she's saying this. She doesn't even look pretty anymore. Her face is all scowly.

"They make him seem like a loser. I'm sorry, but they do. Nobody could believe I was going out with him. None of my friends are going to be friends with him anymore. He probably thinks they will, but they won't."

I'm not sure what to say. I almost want to tell her that Mr. Norris never liked her all that much, but I don't. Instead, I look up and see that George isn't on the lawn anymore. I look down the street, then back up. I don't see him anywhere. I'm holding Lucky's leash, so I can't call the dog to figure out where George is. I turn back to Lisa. "Did you see where George went?"

She turns around to where he was on the lawn, then turns back and shrugs. "No."

She doesn't look nervous, but maybe she doesn't understand that George can't just leave if I'm in charge of him. "I have to find him," I say. We're standing near an intersection, which means he could have gone up any of the four streets. "He doesn't usually wander away unless he hears something like a lawn mower. Or a leaf blower."

I stop and listen. Nothing.

My heart feels like it's bouncing around in my stomach. I move up the street. He isn't anywhere.

When I turn back, I can't believe it. Lisa isn't helping me look, she's staring down at her phone, reading a text. "Can you help me please? I really need to find him." I sound more scared than I mean to. I can't help it. I *am* scared.

I've never lost George before.

"Do you want me to call Martin?" I can tell by her voice, she's not even worried. She just wants to call Martin.

"No," I say. "Martin's back home. What can he do from there?"

I think about what our mom does when George gets lost. Usually she doesn't panic at first. She says you have to think like George and remember what was on his mind when he wandered away. "He was talking about Santa Claus," I say out loud.

Lisa gives me a funny look to remind me that George is too old for Santa. "He loves Christmas," I explain.

She looks more confused. What does this have to do with where he might have wandered off to? I can't explain, so I don't bother. *"George!"* I call again from the middle of the intersection. The problem when George gets lost is that he never answers when he's called. He gets too interested in whatever he's looking at or listening to. Once we lost him for almost an hour on a picnic in the woods. Finally we found him next to an anthill, poking it with a stick. He hadn't been that far away. He just hadn't realized he should have called back.

"George, if you hear me, say here I am!" I scream, then stop and listen.

Nothing.

"Don't you want to use my phone?" Lisa offers. "You could call your mom? Or the police?"

He's been missing for maybe ten minutes now. I'm not going to do either one of those things. "Just forget it, Lisa. I'll look myself. You can go home."

Apparently she's been waiting for me to say this because she sticks her phone in her pocket and says, "Okay, I probably should. I'm sure my mom is wondering where I am."

I look at her and can't believe it: she doesn't care about George, or me. A minute later, she's gone.

I walk up one street, calling George's name. I look down the driveways where he might have wandered if something in a garage caught his eye. This is the other problem with George. He has no sense of personal space or private property. He'll wander into people's garages, whether we know them or not.

I look for open ones that he might have gone into. "George?" I call into one.

"Who?" a gruff voice answers.

There's an old man bent over his toolbox, standing in the back.

"Sorry!" I say. "I'm looking for my brother."

"He's not here."

"Okay."

I go back to the corner where I first lost him and start to get *really* scared. It's getting cold outside and windy, too. Leaves are blowing into the street, which makes me more scared. That's another thing George loves. He follows blowing leaves sometimes.

Lucky pulls at the leash in the direction of our house, but I can't go back without George. I hold my breath and listen again.

Nothing.

"George!" I scream, standing at the corner where I was talking to Lisa. I run up another street in the opposite direction. *"Lisa!"* I can't believe she ran off and left me without helping. Or maybe I should believe it. Maybe that's what Martin and Mr. Norris were trying to tell me.

Up ahead I see something that makes me even more afraid: there's a house where someone has left the front door open. George loves open front doors. They're his favorite thing about Halloween. He thinks it means he's welcome to walk inside, which he always used to do until Mom and Dad made a rule: no walking past the candy bowl ever.

Now there's just an open door and no candy bowl to stop him.

If he came this direction and saw this front door, he would definitely walk inside.

I already know what would happen if a stranger screamed at him for being inside their house: he'd start to giggle. He always does when he's in trouble, and it makes everything worse. No one understands why George laughs when everyone is angry at him. I go up to the porch of the house with the open door and call softly, "George?"

I hear voices inside.

I call again. "George? Are you in there?"

Another terrible thought occurs to me. If he knows he's in trouble at home—really big trouble—George will hide, sometimes for hours.

It's happened once before. He got so angry when the computer crashed that he stomped on the mouse and cracked it into pieces. Then he felt so bad, he hid in the basement behind the boiler. When we finally found him, he'd fallen asleep there and wet his pants. He wasn't giggling nervously then. That time, he just cried and cried until finally Mom and Dad put him to bed. I wonder if George might be in this family's basement, too scared to say anything or get himself out.

I have to ring their doorbell and ask. I have no choice. It's my fault if he's down there. I shouldn't have gotten distracted talking to Lisa. I should have kept my eye on him.

A woman comes to the door. She's my mother's age, but she's got blond hair and she's more dressed up than my mother ever gets. She's wearing pearls and a light-blue sweater.

"Yes?" she says.

Behind her, I hear a weird sound. Maybe the TV is on because it sounds like someone crying. I can tell the woman is surprised to see the door open. She looks at me funny like maybe I opened it.

"I'm sorry to disturb you," I say. Something about this woman is scary. My voice is shaking. "I've lost my brother and I noticed your door open. Sometimes he walks inside a house if a door is open."

She makes a face like someone should teach my brother better manners. "How old is he?" she says.

I can tell she expects me to say three or maybe four. "Twelve," I say. "But he's autistic. I'm so sorry."

She steps out on the porch. "And you think he might be *inside* our house?"

"I'm so sorry. I should have kept a better eye on him. It's my fault."

"You know kids shouldn't walk into other people's houses."

"Yes, I know."

"I don't care what he's got, someone better teach him that."

I'm surprised by how mean she sounds. Usually when you tell people George is autistic, they at least pretend to be understanding.

"I know," I say. "We're trying."

"If he walks into someone's house, they could think he

was a burglar and shoot him. It's allowed, you know."

I wish I could disappear. "He's never done it before. It's possible he's not in your house at all." I sound stupid. We're George's family, which means we know him best, but if you don't have autism, it's impossible to understand the way George thinks.

I wish this woman would be more understanding. I'm a kid who made a mistake. If she'd let me in her house, I could look around for two minutes and see if George is here. It wouldn't take me long. I could guess where he might hide. I think about asking her if I can just look around her basement for two minutes, then I'd be done and she wouldn't have to worry about me or my brother anymore.

But before I ask, I see a surprise: Lisa is standing behind her. Apparently, this is *her* porch I'm standing on. And *her* mean mother I'm talking to.

"What are *you* doing here?" Lisa says, not very nice.

"I'm still looking for George. I can't find him." I can't help it. My voice is back to shaking. Maybe I just want her to understand it's a little bit her fault, too. She was standing there when he walked away from us. If she hadn't distracted me, I would have seen which street he went up at least.

"He's back at your house. I just talked to Martin. They're

wondering where you are."

She stares at me funny, like she can't believe I don't know this, but how was I supposed to know it if I've spent the last half hour running around looking for him?

"Did you tell them what I was doing?"

"No. I wasn't thinking about it because Martin and I just broke up for good. We're not speaking anymore so I couldn't call him back and tell him." She takes a deep breath and shuts her eyes, like she's trying not to cry. "That's all, Benny. I sort of forgot about you. Sorry."

She says it so fast, I can't believe her mother doesn't make her apologize again, only this time sound like she means it, please.

But she doesn't.

Instead they look at each other like maybe her mother has just been saying, *Martin's family is strange. I don't think you should get involved with any of them.*

I don't know what I'm waiting for except maybe to have someone say something nice.

No one does.

SIXTEEN

BACK AT HOME, MARTIN IS AT the kitchen counter, telling our mother what Lisa said to him. "She says she feels sorry for any girl I marry if I ever get it together enough to marry anyone."

Mom can't help but smile. "Does she remember that you're only in the ninth grade?"

"I think so. I'm not sure. It's possible she forgot."

An hour ago, I would have been furious at Martin for making fun of Lisa, who apparently I loved more than he ever did. Now I'm sort of grateful. When they see me, Mom holds out her arms. "There you are! We couldn't figure out what happened to you."

I tell them I thought I'd lost George. Then I tell them the

whole story of running into Lisa and what her mother said to me.

"Her mother is a piece of work," Martin says. "She gets dressed up and puts on makeup to go to the grocery store."

Our mother is a landscape designer, which means she goes to other people's gardens and digs around in their dirt. Usually she'll wash her hands before she goes to the grocery store, but sometimes she forgets even that and shops with mud in her fingernails. She might be messier than Lisa's mother, but if a kid came to her door saying he'd lost his brother, our mother wouldn't stand there asking him questions. She'd turn around and say, *Let's find this kid.*

Then George walks in, talking to his hand. I'm so grateful to see him, I go over and hug him. "You should have told me you were going home, George," I say. "You made me run all around like a chicken with no head, looking for you."

George laughs and bounces up and down. He loves that expression—a chicken with no head. Then he sees Martin and his whole face changes, like a cloud has blown in. "No more Lisa Lowes," he says. "That's it!"

Recently George has started doing something a little different. He doesn't repeat exactly what you say but something you *could* have said. Or *thought* about saying. I think it means George understands a little more than we think. We all watch him as he paces back and forth, finishing his monologue.

"I said that's it, Lisa Lowes! No more! I'm going home! Bye-bye!"

I don't think he realizes we're listening.

"George," Mom says. "It's okay. Benny's home now. Everything's fine."

And then it occurs to me—he isn't repeating anything either Martin or I said. He remembers Lisa Lowes. He said her name first when we ran into her today. He's noticed pretty girls all his life, but this year he's noticed them a lot more. He'll sit close to one in assembly and try to touch her sleeve. Or he'll lean over, close his eyes, and sniff her hair. If I'm nearby, I'll say, *"George!"* and he knows to back away. He knows he shouldn't get too close to pretty girls, but he can't help it sometimes. The sparkly things they wear, the way they smell.

Usually it's so hard to imagine what George is thinking about that it never occurs to me—maybe he's thinking about the same things we are. Maybe he was a little in love with Lisa Lowes, too. Maybe we all were, for a while anyway.

Mom must be thinking the same thing I am. "Oh, Georgie," she says. She puts one arm around me and holds the other one out for George to flutter into. "Did you like Lisa?" she whispers into the top of his head.

"Don't know!" he says.

"I did!" I say, because I'm hoping pretty soon we can make this a joke. "I liked her so much I tried to read *Little House on the Prairie*."

"Wow," Martin says, shaking his head. "How did that go?"

"Not great. I kept waiting for the locusts to come in but they never did. The part I read was all bread baking and laundry and stuff like that."

"Right." Mom sighs. "If only there were more locust plagues in our lives. Then things would be more interesting."

George has wiggled away and gone over to the sofa, where Dad is sitting watching all this. I look over in his direction, hoping he doesn't ruin the moment by suggesting bike riding at the track again. I haven't told Mom about him saying this. It's too sad, especially when he seems so much better sometimes. Then I look at George, bent over right in front of Dad, like he's trying to smell his breath.

"George?" I say. "What are you doing?"

He backs away and I see: Dad's face is empty. His eyes are open, but something is wrong. He's not blinking or moving.

"Brian?" Mom says, moving closer. Then she screams, *"Brian!"* Just touching him is enough for her to know. "Call nine one one," she says.

I wonder how long Dad has been sitting here like this, before George looked over and saw what the rest of us didn't.

SEVENTEEN

I DON'T WANT TO TALK TO ANYONE at school. I especially don't want to talk to Jeremy, who says, first thing when he sees me the next morning, "Did you see I got another footprint?"

"I don't care about stupid footprints," I say so loud that the girls at the other table look over. I don't care. I only came to school this morning because Mom made me. She said I had to come and look after George.

Martin is with her at the hospital, which is where I want to be, too, but she couldn't deal with George all day at the hospital. He had to come to school, so she asked me to please come to school with him.

On the bus, George laughed like he always does, because

he might have been the first one to notice something was happening with Dad, but he doesn't understand what it means.

I don't want to tell anyone at school. I don't want to talk about how an ambulance came last night just like last time, only this time felt different. Mom didn't look at us at all or worry about what we'd do if she left us alone. This time she looked only at Dad and held his hand the whole time they were putting him on the stretcher and taking him.

She climbed inside the ambulance and told Martin, "I'll call you when we get there."

By the time she finally called, we were up in bed. Martin said we could all sleep in George's room the way we do on Christmas Eve. He brought in the blow-up mattress and lay on it, with all his clothes on, saying it was probably a good thing that Mom hadn't called. I knew that wasn't true of course.

When she finally called, she told us that Dad was still alive, which was the good news. The bad news was that he'd had another brain bleed and he was going to need another surgery. The doctors told her he still might die but there was an equal chance that he wouldn't. We should stay positive, she said. She promised she'd come home and be there in the morning.

All day at school I think about Dad's scar and the hair that has finally started to grow around it. Every day I've been watching his hair get a little bit longer, hoping that if he looks more like his old self maybe he'll start to *be* his old self, too. Now when he wakes up from this surgery—*if* he wakes up from this surgery—we'll be back at the beginning again. He'll probably have a new bumpy scar somewhere on his head and he'll shout things no one understands because brain surgeries make you paranoid and mad.

If he wakes up. Last time, we didn't worry about him dying. He was fine after the accident on the track, walking around and talking. How do you die if you were *fine* ten minutes before? After we hung up last night, I got mad that Mom told us how bad this could be. Martin said it was better to know. "She wants us to be ready for whatever happens, that's all."

Be ready for Dad *dying*? How does anyone get ready for that?

Certainly George doesn't bother trying. On the bus ride here, he did the same thing he always does, which is sit behind Taro, the driver, because he likes watching him work the gearshift and the pedals. When we walked into school, I knew Ms. Bartholomew, the art teacher, didn't know anything because she smiled big at George and said, "Who's going to have a good day today?" I hate when teachers treat George like he's in kindergarten but he obviously doesn't mind so most of them do. *"I am!"* he said, giving her a high five and laughing.

I wanted to tell Ms. Bartholomew that George will *not* have a good day. Neither of us will, maybe for the rest of the year. Or even the rest of our lives.

"You want to know how I got my footprint?" Jeremy whispers. "'Cause it was easy. It was so easy it was stupid."

"I don't want to know," I say. I put my face in my hands. I'm afraid I might start to cry.

"What you do is, you go into the office and you ask Ms. Champoux if she'd like a refill on her coffee. That's it. A little milk and one sugar and, bam, I got us another footprint."

He likes pretending he's doing this for the class, not himself, which is one more irritating thing about Jeremy.

Then it's strange. It seems like Mr. Norris is having as bad a day as I am. He's forgotten everything—including our spelling tests—at home. "I even forgot my lunch," he says, shaking his head when he looks at the empty lunch box he accidentally brought.

I know that Mr. Norris's bad day doesn't have to do with me. This morning, Martin asked me what we should tell the school, and I said we should wait until we know what's going to happen to Dad. I didn't want everyone looking at me with hopeful expressions on their faces, like they wanted to say, *Fingers crossed! Let's hope he lives!* So Mr. Norris can't be thinking about me when he breaks a pencil during math time, and later when he closes a desk drawer on his finger so badly he asks Amelia to get him a cup of ice from the nurse.

He's tired and he's thinking about his own problems. That's why I haven't gotten any footprints. I wish I could write him an anonymous note with my mother's favorite tip: *When bad things happen, think about someone else's problems and try to help them.*

By this, I would mean: he should think about me! He should think about how I've been a nice kid all year and now that my dad might be dying, he should sit down with a big stack of footprints and write up a bunch with my name on them. Maybe that would help him feel better.

By the end of the day, I know that's a stupid idea. Mom said she'd call the school if there was any big news, which she hasn't done, so I have to assume that at least there isn't *bad* news.

I should feel relieved, but instead I feel mad. What if every day is like this for the rest of the year—where I spend the whole time wondering if I'll be a half orphan when I go home? It's not Dad's fault, I know, but I hate him for not being able to fix it like he used to fix everything around the house.

I hate him for not acting like himself for so long—for sounding like a kid or a strange, angry drunk person sometimes. I hate him for getting all our hopes up and seeming better and then getting a brain bleed again. It's the one thing I've learned in fourth grade so far: there's nothing I should count on being happy about. I was so happy when I got Mr. Norris, who was fun for a while, until he got so distracted and wasn't fun anymore. Then I was happy when I found out I hadn't lost George and we were all home with Dad, laughing about Lisa.

And now this.

I definitely have to get better at not counting on anything, I think.

I can't help myself—I'm so scared to go home, I start crying a little bit when I get on the bus in the afternoon. I slouch down in my seat so my backpack rides up and no one can see what's happening with my eyes. That's when I look up and notice the front seat behind Sue, our afternoon bus driver, is empty. The bus ahead of us is leaving and she's pulling the door shut.

I grab my backpack and start up to the front of the bus.

"Wait!" I say. Usually, an aide or one of the assistant principals stands with George until he gets on the bus, but they don't always keep perfect track of him because usually they don't have to. George loves riding the bus. He knows our bus number and our driver. He's never made a mistake about this. Usually he's the first person on.

"I need to get off," I say.

Sue gives me a tired look in her mirror. She's not as nice as Taro, our morning driver. "I forgot something," I say, because I see George on the far side of the playing fields, wearing his backpack. He's near the bushes where soccer balls get lost sometimes, but George doesn't care about soccer balls. I have no idea what he's doing over there. "I can't wait for you," Sue says. "All the buses are pulling out."

"I know," I say. George is too far away for me to tell what he's doing, but I have a terrible feeling I know what happened. Mom called the school in the last hours to tell them Dad is dead. They told George but not me because maybe

Mr. Norris didn't answer a page. George knows and ran away to cry in the bushes. Somehow he got away, because suddenly he's better at sneaking off. I should know. He did it to me yesterday.

"It's fine if you leave without me," I tell Sue. I'm scared if she doesn't open the door and let me off, I'll start to really cry. "Just let me off," I say. "Please."

I catch one break at least. I get off the bus just as a late class of third graders comes out of the building. Mr. Wilder, the principal, is too busy shuffling kids onto their buses to notice me running away from mine. I run as fast as I can across the field to George, but it's hard, running and crying at the same time. My heart is beating and I'm afraid of what I'll hear when I get to him: *Dad's dead! No more Dad!*

I hate this. I hate Mom for making us come to school today. I hate Dad for getting sick. I hate Martin for being at the hospital, where we should all be right now.

By the time I get to George, I'm a mess and I almost can't believe it. George isn't crying, he's laughing and pointing at a hole in the bushes. He's rocking back and forth, flapping his hands a little. "It's Mr. Norris's path! Mr. Norris says, Bye, George."

He's right. It's the shortcut path to Mr. Norris's apartment building. The one he used to use every morning until he started driving his beat-up car to work. George remembers weird things like this. Maybe he even notices that it's been weeks since he's seen Mr. Norris walk through these bushes, carrying a cookie sheet full of snacks for the class. Maybe this is his way of asking what's going on. Who knows with George, but for the moment I'm so relieved he's not telling me Dad is dead that I laugh and look where he's pointing his stick. Just beyond the bushes is the path that dips down into a drainpipe and comes up again in the back of a parking lot for the apartment complex. Because it's still the middle of the day, there aren't too many cars in the lot.

Then I see a real surprise: Mr. Norris's car pulls into the parking lot. George recognizes it, too. He bounces up and down and squeals a little in excitement. "Shh, George," I say. "We're just going to watch."

In the distance, I see the last three buses close their doors and pull away. Now we'll have to go to the office and call home for a ride. Maybe somewhere in the back of my mind, I'm thinking: *the longer we put off going home, the longer we won't have to hear any bad news about Dad.* I push George ahead of me so we're on the path, hidden by the bushes, and no one will look over here and wonder what we're doing.

EIGHTEEN

I'M NOT SURE WHY IT'S NEVER occurred to me to spy on Mr. Norris and figure out the reason he's changed so much recently. He's right here. It would have been so easy. Maybe he's working another job on the side. Maybe he's not doing anything except playing video games all the time. Maybe Mom is right and video games really do rot your brain and make you forget things.

It's hard for George to be quiet. He has to make sounds even if I've told him to be quiet. He can't really help himself.

"Shh," I say. "We can't let him see us. We're just looking, George, okay?"

We watch Mr. Norris get out of his car. He walks around

to the back and opens the trunk to pull out a box. I can feel George about to explode beside me. He wants to scream, *Hi, Mr. Norris!* Or *We're over here!* He's terrible at hide-and-seek because he always wants to be found. I squeeze his elbow and whisper, "You have to be *quiet,* George."

I'm not even sure what I'm hoping to see or why spying on Mr. Norris seems like a good way to forget our other problems. I try to figure out what's in the box. It looks lightweight, like maybe it's got clothes. Then there's another surprise: Mr. Norris opens the back door of the car. Whoever's in there must be a kid, but Mr. Norris doesn't have children. Or at least not any that he's mentioned to us.

The person who gets out doesn't seem like a kid at first. He's as tall as Mr. Norris and wears a sweatshirt with the hood up so we can't see his face. His clothes are kind of messy, and his elastic-waist pants are twisted to one side. Everything about him is a little off. He's got the start of a mustache and a candy necklace. Then I put together a few clues: he's wearing Velcro-strap shoes like George's, plus he's standing on his toes and fidgeting with a rubber-band bracelet in his hand.

George can't take the excitement of all this: seeing Mr. Norris with someone who reminds him of himself. *"What are you doing in the bushes?"* he shouts.

I try to put my hand over his mouth, but I'm too late. It's what he wants Mr. Norris to say. Like this is all a game, and pretty soon we'll be laughing.

"Who's over there?" Mr. Norris squints in our direction. "Benny, is that you?"

I don't have any choice now. I have to stand up because George is out of the bushes, bouncing around. "I'm sorry, Mr. Norris," I say, standing up from my hiding spot. "I had to come over here to get George. He didn't get on the bus today—he came over here instead. I don't know why."

"Yeah, I talked to him at recess today. He asked if he could come over after school."

He did? George is always capable of surprising us, but this *really* surprises me. "Why?"

"I don't know. I told him it wasn't a good idea," he says loudly. "Didn't I, George?"

George ignores him and bounces over to the trash Dumpster.

"He shouldn't have done this, Mr. Norris. I'm sorry. I'll take him back to school and we'll call home for a ride."

"No, Benny. Why don't you come to my apartment and we'll call your folks from there." I can tell by the way he says "folks" that he doesn't know my dad is back in the hospital. I follow him back toward the car. "I can also introduce you to my son, Aaron."

My voice is almost a whisper now. "I didn't know you had a son."

"Usually he lives with his mother during the week and stays with me on weekends, but a few weeks ago his grandmother had a stroke. Aaron's mom had to go to Arizona to take care of her so Aaron's been with me full-time."

I think about the changes I've noticed and the clues I've been trying to piece together.

"Aaron doesn't do well with changes to his routine. Two weeks ago, he bit a girl on his van. Badly enough that he's not allowed to ride on it for a while. I've had to drive him to school myself and pick him up, which is why I've been late to class a few times." We're standing away from Aaron, where he can't hear us.

This explains a lot of things—why he's been distracted and tired. Why *So B. It* made him sad. We start walking toward his apartment.

"Aaron's not as high functioning as George. He can only say a few words and sometimes he can be aggressive. Because of that, he has to go to a special school."

"Oh." I nod. "Okay."

I've never thought of George as being higher functioning than anyone else. There are so many things George can't do: tie his shoes. Cut his pancakes. Zip his jacket. Once, I tried to help him with his math homework, which was measurements. He never got the idea that you have to line up one end of the ruler with one end of the thing. He just waved the ruler around and said everything was three inches because George likes to get homework done as quickly as possible so he can watch his videos on YouTube.

When I told Mom that I didn't think he'd really gotten the idea of measuring, she said, "It's okay, honey. I don't think he ever will." That made me sad. Like George might never change. When I told Mom later, she said it was okay to feel sad for a little while but we shouldn't stay sad for too long because George was mostly happy and part of being George's family is just accepting him. I wonder how hard that is with someone who bites girls on vans.

"You know, Benny, I was surprised when you said I never noticed you at school. I watch you with your brother all the time. It always makes me wish Aaron had a little brother who would talk to him on the playground and be friends with him. I sometimes wonder if he'd be different if he had that." I can tell this conversation is making Mr. Norris sad. "That's probably why I haven't given you a footprint. Because I don't think one little sentence could describe all that I see you do for him."

Now I'm really worried that he might start crying, so I turn away and look at George, who has found some gravel to dribble on the other side of the Dumpster.

Aaron stands near his apartment door, eating his candy necklace.

"I probably should have told you all this, I know. My ex-wife never wanted us to talk about Aaron's diagnosis with people outside the family. She thought unpleasant subjects shouldn't be discussed. I suppose I'm used to thinking that way. I knew you were coming into my class this year and I know George, of course. I thought about saying something the first day when we all introduced ourselves, and then I wondered about all the students I'd had before who I never talked about Aaron with. I worried that it would make them feel like they hadn't really known me."

I think of Lisa. Even though I don't like her anymore, I think of how important he still is to her, four years after she left his class. How surprised she'd be if I told her.

"You've taught me something this year, Benny. You might not even realize it."

Whatever it is, he's right. I don't realize.

"I've figured out that having something big that you don't talk about adds a lot of stress to your life. It made me feel like I was keeping a secret and I would have been better off from the start telling the truth to the whole class. That I have a pretty disabled son temporarily living with me during the week. You all would have understood, I'm sure. And maybe it would have made you feel a little less lonely, right, Benny?"

"Yeah," I whisper. I almost say, *I've been keeping a secret, too.* I want to tell him: *My dad's back in the hospital again. We're here because we're scared to go home and find out what's happening.*

I can't get the words out, though.

I'm crying and nothing will come out of my mouth. He comes over and hugs me, which makes George start laughing nervously. "You're a strong kid, Benny," he says. "Stronger than you probably realize."

I manage to stop crying and wipe my face. "Thanks, Mr. Norris."

It's strange to get inside his apartment and see everything about Mr. Norris's life up close. Like unwashed cereal bowls in the sink. And books folded open on the sofa. It looks nothing like I imagined it would—full of video games and toys. By the look of it, he's like my parents, who are a little messy and read a lot.

Mr. Norris tells us to sit down on the sofa, while he looks for the phone, because it isn't in the cradle where it should be. "It never is," he says, laughing a little. "I'd blame Aaron except that he doesn't use the phone."

I can tell he's trying to joke with someone who will understand, which I do. George has never made a phone call in his life.

"I'll call the school, so they can call your folks and see about getting a ride for you."

Mr. Norris goes to use the phone in the bedroom, leaving me alone with Aaron, who looks very nervous, and George, who won't sit down no matter how many times I tell him to. Any time George is in an unfamiliar place, he always looks around in ways that aren't polite. He likes opening doors and cupboards. Sometimes he'll open refrigerators and look in people's Tupperware. Once he starts doing it, it's impossible to stop him. If you try, he'll start crying or screaming really loud, so I don't bother until I look over at Aaron and see how nervous George is making him. I wish

I had a magic trigger I could pull that would stop George in his tracks.

Aaron stands by the front door with his fingers in his ears.

When George opens the bathroom door and goes inside to test the echo of his singing voice, Aaron starts moving around the edge of the room, making a high-pitched squeaking sound, getting more and more nervous.

"George, you need to get out of there," I say. "Come out here and sit next to me."

"No thank you!"

"Please, George. I'll brush my teeth with my finger!"

"No thank you!"

George laughs like he thinks it's funny that Aaron is so scared of him. Dad used to say that George likes seeing other autistic kids because he gets ideas for new stims from them. Stims are the things autistic kids do over and over for no reason, like bouncing and flapping their hands, which is George's favorite. But if he's around other autistic kids, he'll borrow new stims for a while. He'll squeak or roll his eyes backward or wiggle his fingers in his peripheral vision. All of them make him look pretty weird.

Now I'm pretty sure George will get home and circle our living room with his fingers in his ears because he's spent the last ten minutes watching Aaron do it. Aaron's up on his toes now, like if we don't leave soon he might explode. He starts making a high-pitched whine that maybe only I can hear, because Mr. Norris doesn't come running.

George hears it, too, and laughs more. Then he makes everything ten times worse by following Aaron around in his frantic living room circle.

"George, stop it right now!" I scream.

He doesn't stop.

"I'll tell Mom to take away your screen!"

He still doesn't stop and Mr. Norris doesn't come back.

I don't know what to do. And then I notice a book, lying on the floor next to the coffee table: *The Night Before Christmas*. I can't believe it's out already. For the rest of the world, it isn't Halloween yet, but in autism world, I guess, it's Christmas all year round. This one is George's favorite, mostly because it stars George's favorite person, Santa. "George, look!" I say. "It's *The Night Before Christmas*!"

George stops following Aaron and comes over to the sofa. I'm grateful to have stopped him, but I'm not sure if it will last. "Read it, Benny," he says, bending close so he can look at the pictures from an inch away.

"You have to sit down first," I say.

He doesn't sit.

"Read it!"

"Not until you sit down."

He does. I open the book and put my arm through his so he won't get back up. I start to read: "''Twas the night before Christmas when all through the house not a creature was stirring, not even a . . .'" I wait. This is an old game Dad used to play. "A camel?"

"Mouse!" they both shout.

I can't believe it. Aaron is still circling the room, but he said it, too. He talked.

Dad used to do this when George made him read the same Dr. Seuss books over and over. He'd change a few words to pretty funny things that made us all laugh. Now it makes me feel great. I got Aaron to speak!

I keep going. "'Mama in her kerchief, and I in my cap, had just settled for a long winter's' . . . cup of cocoa."

"Nap!" they both shout.

George bounces next to me on the sofa. At least he's not scaring Aaron anymore, though it's hard to tell if Aaron is enjoying this game or if it's making him more nervous to hear this poem wrong. I keep going for a while, saying some lines right and some wrong. And then I look behind me and see Mr. Norris standing there, watching us and holding the phone.

I stop reading when I see the expression on his face. "I just talked to your mom," he says. "There's some news about your dad."

NINETEEN

I THINK: *This is what people look like when they tell you that your dad is dead.* His face is white and his eyes don't blink. He looks like he isn't even breathing.

I think: *If I hear it from him, I'll always remember it this way.* That I got to know him better and then he had to tell me my dad is dead.

It's too big for me to take it all in. The first thing I think is: *Dad dying just ruined this great thing I did, getting Aaron to talk.* The second thing is: *Dad dying means I can't like Mr. Norris anymore, I'll have to hate him now.*

I start to cry. A loud, terrible, stupid cry that makes me feel worse because I don't even know if I'm crying for Dad or because of Mr. Norris.

Mr. Norris rushes over and sits down next to me. He puts an arm around my shoulder and tells me he's sorry, this must be so hard for me. He says he had no idea my dad was back in the hospital. "You should have told me," he says. "I wish I'd known. I would have understood what George was talking about at recess today."

I calm down enough to breathe and wipe my face and ask, "What did George say?"

"He asked if he could come over to my house after school. He said he couldn't go home."

I look over at where George is now standing, staring up at a vent fan over the stove in the kitchen. I should remember what Mom said. *George always surprises us. He might think every object in the world is three inches long, but he understands some things better than we think.* He doesn't want to go back to a house without Dad. That's why he didn't get on the bus. He felt the same way I did. He even made a plan.

Just imagining it starts me crying all over again. Mr. Norris squeezes my shoulder and pats my back. "Hey, buddy, your dad's okay. The news is he woke up. He hasn't said anything yet, but he squeezed your mom's hand and blinked to answer questions. All good signs. She sounded pretty happy just now."

I can't believe it. "You talked to her?"

"Yes. That's why I was taking so long. I'm sorry about that. She's also worried about both of you. She's at the hospital, but a friend already drove Martin home to meet you off the bus and tell you what's going on."

I roll my eyes so he knows: one of us might be autistic but we know how to walk home from the bus stop.

We're not little kids anymore.

TWENTY

THE HOSPITAL IS WEIRD BUT LESS scary than last time. At least we know it now. We know where the bathrooms are and the elevators and the cafeteria. We know the nurses will mostly smile at us and usually make a fuss. Mom says this is because they work twelve-hour shifts and don't get to see their own kids enough so they're happy to see other people's.

Five days after his surgery, though, Dad still isn't talking. Except for that part, he seems more like his old self than I would have expected. He makes pantomime jokes and funny faces about the food. He's on a restricted diet, so nothing has salt or any flavor. "It's all Jell-O and clear soups," Mom says. "Poor Dad."

To help him out, we think of a plan. On our second visit to the hospital, Martin puts a box of saltine crackers in George's backpack. Ordinarily backpacks aren't allowed on the floor Dad's on. We also have to wear masks and gloves because I guess the patients on this floor are one germ away from dying. It seems strange to wear a surgical mask when we're still wearing our dirty shoes and regular clothes. Mom says technically it's not required, it's an extra precaution, like how everyone in China wears face masks on the subway.

George, who loves coming to the hospital, bounces all the way to Dad's room, still wearing his backpack. All the nurses smile and say hello. No one stops him. No one points to the backpack and says, "Remember? That goes in the locker downstairs." It's one of the pluses to having George. He's already breaking a lot of rules, so who's going to notice one more?

When Dad sees the saltines box, his whole face smiles and then he lets out this new croaky laugh he has. It makes Mom laugh, too, to see him so happy over something we did without telling her. George is so happy he forgets the rule about not playing with Dad's bed and presses the button to raise his feet.

Dad's face goes red with laughing. Finally Mom says,

"Take it easy, Brian."

Mom says this whole business with Dad reminds her of when George was little. "You don't think you could ever, in a million years, handle it, and then it happens and you do. You just go one day at a time and suddenly you realize, here I am. I'm handling it."

Dad comes home two weeks later. He's going to spend days in a rehab center and nights and weekends at home with us. It's an experimental program. They think some patients get better faster if they don't live at a rehab center. It's more work on Mom but she says it's fine as long as we don't mind getting ourselves ready for school in the morning. Now Martin and I make all three lunches, which definitely has its pluses. Mom is too busy, I guess, to notice the jumbo jar of marshmallow fluff Martin bought for us.

Seeing Dad at home, though, makes me realize how different he is now. He still can't talk, but he can write a few words and communicate in other ways. It takes a while, but he does it. Strangely, George is the person who usually understands what he's trying to say first. Of course sometimes he's completely wrong. Once Dad was on the sofa with one hand up in the air. "Ehh . . . tahe," he kept saying. "Ehh . . . tahe."

"Dad wants *E.T.*!" George screamed, which was totally wrong. We never figured out what he wanted that time. When we got him paper and a pen he scribbled only *SORRY*.

Sometimes George is exactly right though. Dad will be on the sofa, touching his ears first, then his chest, and George will run and put on a CD of classical music. And Dad will smile, close his eyes, and lean back happily.

There was another time when Mom had moved the TV up from the basement into the living room so we could all watch together with Dad on the sofa. It was nice of her except then she kept saying we had to find something on the Discovery or History Channel. Which would have been okay except the Discovery Channel was a show on coral reefs and the History Channel was about the development of the printing press. We begged Mom to let us watch something good. She said if we hung in there, the shows would get more interesting and if they didn't, then we should just eat our pizza and be quiet. She was kind of kidding (I think), but still it made us mad. Then Dad dropped his pizza on his plate and said something that sounded like "Fang goo . . ."

He was obviously trying to say something, we just couldn't tell what. "Fang goo, Brian?" Mom said. "What's fang goo?"

Martin nodded and held his hand up like he understood. "It's the stuff vampires use to put their teeth on in the morning, right Dad? It's cool. We understand. Maybe we won't run out tonight, but we'll get some for you tomorrow. Fang goo, Mom. Put it on your shopping list."

"Martin, stop," Mom said. "What do you want, Brian?"

Dad tried again. "Fang goo!" he screamed, except this time he smiled like he was making a joke. He didn't look at Mom though. He looked at each of us. I kept thinking, *This is a joke. He's trying to make an old Dad joke,* but I couldn't figure out what it was.

And then George did.

"Family Guy," George said, rocking back and forth. "*Family Guy* is on."

Dad held up his hand to high-five George. Mom rolled her eyes and then laughed. In the old days *Family Guy* was the cause of some terrible fights between them. We were too young, Mom always said, especially me. Mom would really yell at him, "We agree on this and then I come home and George is quoting lines from it! I mean it! I really don't want them watching that show. I'm not just saying this!"

We can all remember the fights, which made it seem funnier now that we've got bigger problems to worry about.

Mom stood up with her hands on her hips. "Is that really going to be your first sentence, Brian? Really? *Family Guy*?"

He was laughing like a kid then, so Martin filled in with what Dad used to say. "The humor is sophisticated, Mom. It's teaching us about satire."

"Oh please," Mom said and went to the kitchen to make popcorn.

Now it's been like this for a while and we've gotten into a routine. School is going okay. There's one week left in the footprint contest and I've changed my strategy. In the cafetorium at lunch I don't crawl around on the floor to pick up trash. Instead of trying to be perfect, I'm trying to be myself. Which means after lunch I go over to the computer room, where I can sign up for fifteen minutes of computer time to work on my Lego movie. I think I have a pretty good idea for how to end my movie. I got it from a scene in *The Indian in the Cupboard* where Omri is having an argument with his friend Patrick, who wanted to bring all his toys to life. Omri only lets him do it to one toy, the funny cowboy named Boone. Omri keeps telling Patrick to remember that they have to be taken care of when they come to life. "These are *people*, not toys."

That's what I have Yoda say to my guys. "People you still are, though look different you do."

I can't have them go back to the scenes from their old movies, because I can't find any clips of those characters waking up or looking around and saying, "Wait—what happened?" If I could, maybe it would work, but since I can't, I have to forget it. These guys have to stay Lego for this four-minute movie. They have no choice, really, which means they have to adapt.

So here's my idea: the last scene of the movie, they're eating dinner (all plastic food they don't like much from my Medieval Village set: little green apples, brown chicken legs, a whole silver fish). They're all pretty depressed until the door opens and they see Lego Chewbacca standing there. He comes in grunting, pulls up a chair, and starts eating. Then the door opens again. There's Princess Leia and Luke Skywalker. Same thing only they can talk. "Oh good!" she says. "You've got apples! And chicken! My favorites!"

It keeps going like that—the door opens, new people walk in—until they've got a room full of every recognizable minifig I could find. Ninja Turtles, SpongeBob, everyone's there, set up in funny poses, talking to one another. Everyone's pretty happy with the plastic food laid out. The point is: it's happened to all of them. They've all turned plastic, they've all got no elbows, they're all a little sick of the stupid holes in their feet, but they've all adjusted.

"You get used to it," SpongeBob tells Count Dooku. "And there's some plus sides. I don't have to act so stupid. When you're not in your old show, you can act however you want."

A few more of them say things like this. In the last thirty seconds of the movie, the party gets a little wacky and a few minifigs start dancing on the table. Senator Palpatine goes to dip Princess Leia and they both end up falling off the table. "Oh, pardon me. Excuse me," they say to each other. (I admit I stole a few bits from *Shrek*.) Also I'll need Olga to dub in Princess Leia's voice. I can do the others but not that one. Otherwise I think it might just be my best movie yet.

TWENTY-ONE

I'VE DECIDED THERE'S THREE MAIN REASONS that school is going okay. One reason is that a few days after we went to Mr. Norris's apartment, I came to school and found a footprint with my name on it in Mr. Norris's handwriting:

Benny Barrows read my son's favorite book aloud and helped him calm down. Thank you, Benny.

After I told my mom the whole story about going to Mr. Norris's apartment, she told me that Mr. Norris and his wife might have had a hard time staying married with the stress of taking care of Aaron, too. "That's not so uncommon. It didn't happen to us, thank heavens, but it happens a lot. Mr.

Norris probably feels isolated. It sounds like they haven't gotten to know many other families with autistic kids."

I wonder if we'll become friends with Mr. Norris.

"Not yet," my mother says when I ask. "We shouldn't try to be friends with him until after this year is over. When you're not in his class, maybe we can invite him and Aaron over."

I nod and feel a little goose-bumpy at the thought. And then I remember one detail I haven't told her. "You want to hear something weird? Aaron likes Santa, too. And he's memorized *The Night Before Christmas* just like George. Isn't that funny?"

"That is funny," Mom says.

"Why do you think autistic kids like Santa so much?" I ask.

She thinks about it. "I don't think they all do. It's probably just a coincidence. Or else they like him because he's a friendly man who does one very predictable, nice thing a year and doesn't talk too much about it in the process."

It's true that George doesn't like people who talk too much. His favorite people at school—the nurse, the janitor—hardly talk at all. Their friendships are all high fives and whistles and little phrases like "Go for the gold!" which

George said a lot during the Winter Olympics. He liked the sound of it, I guess, the same way he likes Santa. Not because of the presents, which George doesn't care about that much. He likes him because he laughs at nothing, which is sort of like George. They both don't make too much sense, but that's okay.

Another reason school is okay now is that a few days after George and I went to Mr. Norris's apartment, Jeremy came up to me and asked if it was true. "Did you really go inside his apartment?" he said.

"Yes," I said.

"So what's it like? Weird, I bet, right?"

I didn't know what he was hoping I'd say. I definitely wasn't going to tell him about Aaron. "No. It was a pretty normal apartment."

"Weren't you scared though?"

"Not really, why?"

"Because you're not allowed inside a teacher's house. It's against the law."

It *is*?

"That's what my mom and dad said. They said you could get in big trouble for that."

Then I had a very strange thought: *Jeremy's jealous of me.*

He's mad that I know things about Mr. Norris he doesn't know. It made me think about next year when we can invite Mr. Norris and Aaron over to our house and be (sort of) family friends.

Then spelling tests won't matter. Neither will progress reports or footprints. Mr. Norris will like my parents and maybe he'll even say it's nice bringing Aaron someplace where he doesn't have to explain everything he does. Mom always says one of the best parts about having George in our family is that no one expects us to be perfect anymore so we don't have to bother pretending. "You can't imagine what a relief that is," she once told me. Maybe, when Martin was her only baby, she tried to be perfect. I don't know. It's hard to picture. Maybe Jeremy's parents are still trying for that.

There's one last big reason I feel better, though I'd never in a million years tell Jeremy this one. A few days after George and I were in Mr. Norris's apartment, I got a card in the mail with his handwriting on the envelope. It was addressed to me and had flowers on the front. Inside he said,

Dear Benny,

Just found this poem. I think it's a lovely one but I don't think I'll share it with the whole class. It might be a little hard for them

to understand. Still, I thought you should have it. It's by a woman named Naomi Shihab Nye. This is only part of the poem:

> *Before you know kindness as the deepest thing inside,*
> *you must know sorrow as the other deepest thing.*
> *You must wake up with sorrow.*
> *You must speak to it till your voice*
> *catches the thread of all sorrows*
> *and you see the size of the cloth.*
> *Then it is only kindness that makes sense anymore.*

At the bottom, he signed it *Sincerely, Mr. Norris.*

I showed it to Mom because I didn't understand it and I wanted her to help me. She read it out loud and started to cry, which made me wonder if maybe I shouldn't have showed it to her. Then she explained: "It's about how hard times make you appreciate kindness and also make you a kinder person, I think."

Oh, I thought. *Okay.*

And that made me feel better, too.

TWENTY-TWO

I'VE ONLY SEEN MOM CRY a few times since Dad came home from the hospital. The first time was reading Mr. Norris's card. The second time she was filling out insurance papers, sitting at Dad's desk. When I walked in, her eyes were red and her cheeks wet. There was no way either one of us could pretend she wasn't crying.

She held out her arms. "Come here, Benny," she said. Hugging someone who's sitting while you're standing is awkward, so we didn't do it for too long. "I'm thinking about how Dad might not work again and I just have to get used to that. Maybe it helps to say it out loud."

Now I want to cry, too. Except for a few years when

George was young and I was a baby, both my parents have always worked. My mom as a landscape designer, my dad as an architect. A couple of times they've worked together on projects and we went to visit them afterward. I know that's what Mom is thinking about now. Never standing again in a space they've both had a hand in designing. That plus money.

I know she's thinking about money, too.

When we stop hugging, she picks up a hospital bill and shakes her head. "Can we pay it?" I ask and I can guess the answer because she doesn't say anything.

In some ways, Dad is better than he was after the first operation. He doesn't nap all the time. His balance is better now. He walks around without a cane or too much help. He reads a little and writes, too. He just can't talk. At all. Which means Mom is right. He won't be able to work. She doesn't want to cry in front of me, so she blows her nose and says, "We just have to get used to it, that's all."

I wonder if having George in our lives will help this happen faster. Or if we'll feel the other way: Like why are we the family that everything bad happens to?

I think about a story my parents used to tell. How George was born with a big red birthmark on one cheek. It was raised and bumpy and so ugly that Dad took all his baby pictures from one side and Mom joined a support group for parents of infants with facial abnormalities. Then the birthmark faded and now she always talks about it like it's a funny story. "Imagine me thinking a birthmark would be George's biggest problem in life."

I used to not understand why that story was funny. Now I think I do. Bigger problems put littler ones in perspective. Worrying about spelling tests and footprints seems stupid when I come home and watch Dad take ten minutes to write down a question he wants to ask me.

Today, he holds the pencil balled up in his fist like we all did in kindergarten. It takes so much concentration his tongue sticks out. After three words he takes a break to think and then writes two more. Finally he shows it to me and I can't believe it:

Want to ride bike at track?

TWENTY-THREE

MOM IS OUTSIDE IN THE GARDEN, digging in her compost heap, when I finally find her and tell her. "Why won't he let this stupid idea go? It's okay if I'm not a great bike rider. Martin said so."

She shakes her head and blows some of her hair out of her face. "I don't know, Benny. I honestly don't. It's something his brain has latched on to, I guess."

"Why would he want to go back to the place where all the bad stuff started?"

"Maybe that's the point. Maybe that's why he can't let go of it."

"I don't ever want to go back there. I'm sorry, but I don't.

It's like he can't stop thinking about it and it makes me feel terrible."

"Oh, Benny, I don't get it either. I'm sorry."

"Even if I tell him there's no way I'm going bike riding at the track—even if I'm really mean about it—he'll probably forget I said it and ask me again tomorrow."

This is the part none of us has wanted to talk about: how bad Dad's memory is. How much he repeats himself. How frustrating and sad it is.

I start to cry and Mom hugs me. She cries a little bit, too.

"It's hard, baby. It really is. I know."

"What if it doesn't change? What'll we do?"

We sit down side by side at the picnic table that's covered in little pinecones and leaves. "I don't know," she says. "Live with it, I guess."

As long as we're having this conversation—as long as I've said this much—I might as well say it all. "What if it's like having two Georges for the rest of our lives?" I don't say the other part I'm thinking: *What if it's worse?* At least with George we don't remember a different person that makes this one seem sad. "It's not fair," I say. I'm crying more now. "You've already had it so hard with George."

"No, Benny, I don't think it's like that. George used to

be hard. The first five years were hard, figuring everything out. But now he's not hard. He's just George."

"But he doesn't change! He's not going to get better."

"Sure he will. A little bit. Maybe he doesn't change a lot, but there's something interesting I've noticed about George. He changes other people. Dad and I were very different before he came along. We worked too hard. We were always worried about getting more clients and growing our business. We were kind of competitive about it, which we thought was fun, but now I look back and I don't think it was. If I had kept working that way, I don't think I would have been very happy."

This isn't the first time I've heard her say this. Now I have to wonder, with all our new money issues, if she really means it. Pretty soon she'll have to be working twice as hard if Dad can't work at all. But she doesn't seem to be thinking about this. "Having George around has changed all of us. It's made you the nicest, most thoughtful fourth grader I know. It's given Martin a certain amount of depth he might not have had otherwise."

I smile. I like when Mom makes fun of Martin.

"I think about this funny habit I developed years ago, trying to teach George about small talk. Whenever he's with me in the grocery store, I force myself to stop and talk to anyone we know, so maybe he'll start to learn, this is how you extend your conversations. So his might go a little longer than his patented ten-second exchanges." She laughs. We both do. "I don't think he's ever gotten better, has he?"

"Not really."

"So I've been having all these conversations over the years and here we are with all these friends around town. Dropping off meals and doing all these nice things."

She's right about this. Some people have actually set up a schedule now where friends sign up for a day to drop food off. Some of the baskets are great—with little wrapped desserts for each of us and a bone for Lucky. "Did you notice the yard?" Mom says. "The soccer team came over and raked the leaves a few days ago."

How did I not notice this? I think about some of the kids on the soccer team, the ones who are really good at soccer. The ones who like my dad but never talk to me.

"These things widen our world, Benny. They make us see that we're part of a bigger community. People *want* to be nice. They *want* to help. Most of the time we're all just too busy to show it. But look around. . . ." She points to the lawn that's been covered in leaves for weeks and now is completely clean. It must have taken hours to do this or else a whole bunch of kids. I can't believe I didn't notice.

"Did Dad see them? Does he know?"

"I don't think so. He was asleep at the time. I've tried to tell him, but I don't think he remembers that the leaves were here. He's still so confused about time and what season it is. He'll get it eventually."

"Is that why he keeps wanting to go back to the track? Because he thinks it's summer?"

"Maybe. I honestly don't know. I know he was happy that morning because you agreed to go. I know he was really proud of you, riding your bike around that track."

"Was he *that* worried about it?" I'm sort of asking a bigger question: *Are you still worried?*

"Not worried, no. He just didn't want you to be scared of things. He didn't want you to back away from something just because it was hard. He did that a lot when he was a kid and he doesn't want his own boys to do the same thing."

"He *did*?" I say. "Like with what?"

"Oh, you've heard the stories. Dad wasn't a particularly great athlete and he got a lot of Cs when he was in high school."

No one's ever told me this before. Cs equal threes, which

means maybe I'm more like my dad than I realize. "How did he become an architect?"

"I don't know. He went to college and figured out what he wanted and worked a lot harder."

"Do you know what grades he got in elementary school?"

She laughs, surprised. "No! I have no idea. Isn't that funny? I think he really liked elementary school, but I have no idea how he did academically. I guess—maybe—" She slaps her hands on her knees and makes a funny face. "Because it doesn't matter all that much in the end." Then she puts her arm around me and pulls me into a sideways shoulder hug. "What matters is working hard and finding things you love."

"I have that!" I say.

I finally got up the courage to show my Lego movie to a few more people. Mom watched it last week and said it was the best one I'd ever made. "I think it might be my favorite Lego movie ever." This isn't saying all that much since Mom has never seen *The Lego Movie*, but still. It was nice of her to say.

Now, she puts her arm around my shoulder again. "It's true, you do," she says.

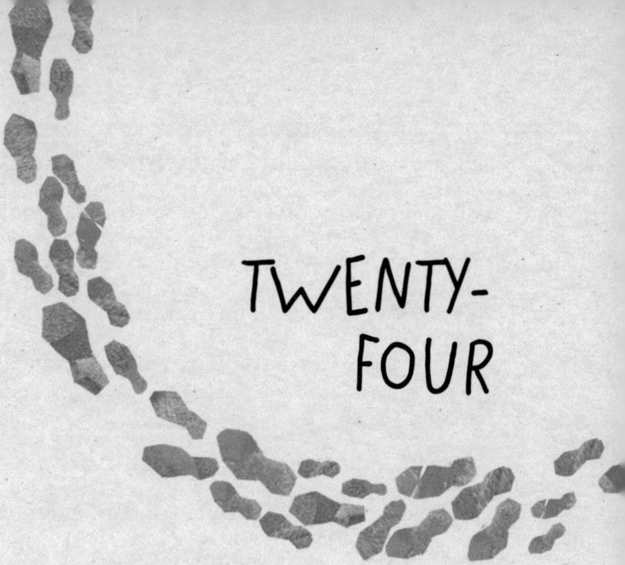

TWENTY-FOUR

THAT NIGHT I KEEP TRYING TO think of solutions even though, right after our talk about money, Mom told me I shouldn't worry about money. "I only told you because I want you to know the truth, but you've already got enough worries on your plate. You don't need to add this one, too. Please, Benny. I mean it."

"Okay," I said.

"Promise me."

"I promise," I said.

Then I spend most of the night sorting through my Lego bins, separating out the smaller items that are sellable on eBay. If you want to get the highest price, the trick is to sell everything individually. After I've collected what I'd consider twenty minifigures with the highest resale value, I take them into Martin's room to get his advice. He knows eBay selling better than I do, but he might point out that most of these were his once, which means he should get all the money.

When I show him the box, I explain it the best I can. "We have to do something, Martin. Mom doesn't have the money to pay all these hospital bills."

Maybe I've told Martin so he'll start thinking of some ways he can pitch in, too. I already know that whatever I make won't be enough. Maybe I also want him to tell me that I shouldn't have to worry about this. Instead he reaches over to the shoe box I've filled with the most valuable pieces I could find. He stirs through the box with his finger. There's a lot in there. Minifigs I bought whole sets to get. Minifigs that have starred or played a role in all of my movies. Minifigs I used to put in my pocket and bring to school back in first and second grade, before I had any friends to eat lunch with or talk to at recess.

"You're really gonna sell these guys?" Martin says.

"I think we have to. We don't have much choice."

I want him to say, *Of course we do. You need these people*

to make your movies. You shouldn't sell them. Instead he says, "You can get twenty dollars apiece for some of these."

"More for a few of them. The original Spider-Man is very rare. One just sold on eBay for forty-five dollars."

He picks it up and turns it over. It doesn't look much different from all the other minifigs, but he's one of the older ones so he's worth more.

I care about Spidey. Even though he wasn't in my latest movie, he's always been my favorite. There was a time when I was young that I couldn't sleep unless he was tucked in my hand. He mattered to me a lot, which made me play weird games with myself. I'd wake up in the morning and hide him somewhere upstairs so I'd have to remember and find him later in the day before I went to bed. It was always a little scary, thinking maybe this time I'd forget where I'd hidden him.

I was that kind of kid, I guess. Before I had real problems, I created some of my own.

Martin's got six guys in one hand, too many to keep looking, so he lays them out on the bed. Penguin, Count Dooku, Princess Leia, two Yodas.

"The Yodas are not as rare as some of the others. They came in too many sets."

He nods. He used to know all this stuff. He was obsessed with Lego for years before I was. He finds more and lays them out. By a generous estimate we could sell all my future cast members and get two hundred dollars.

"That's pretty good, right?"

Martin shakes his head. If making money on these old Lego sets was our end goal, we've made terrible mistakes over the years, throwing away our boxes and all our instruction booklets. We've played too hard with them. We've broken apart every original spaceship and battle tank to make forts and bunkers. We've mixed sets so much that Han Solo and Chewbacca sleep in twin beds from a police headquarters, with a coffeemaker between them.

Now that I look at them lying on Martin's bed, it's hard to imagine putting them into envelopes and sending them off to strangers. I've never told anyone this, but I think of my minifigs as my oldest, truest friends. Because of this, I also think of them as pretty happy time travelers. Han Solo doesn't mind eating medieval food. He's told me, sort of. Or he's given me that impression. I've never told anyone how much I care about them, but all of the sudden, it's like Martin knows.

"You shouldn't sell these, dude." He puts them all back in

the shoe box. "That's not how we're going to do this. Two hundred dollars is chump change. I've got a better idea."

He's moving around his room getting a piece of paper. I follow him, hugging my shoe box because I'll love Martin forever if he can think of a way to spare this box of little plastic best friends.

TWENTY-FIVE

"WE'RE GONNA MAKE A LIST," MARTIN says. "Our top ten moneymakers from the past. We'll see if there's a way to combine them all."

Because our parents never signed us up for camps, we've spent most of our summers around the house, bored and looking for ways to make money. Over the years we've come up with a few decent ones.

Probably our best is the kiddie carnival, which works because there are a lot of kids on our block, most of them much younger than us. To do this, we put flyers in everyone's mailbox and then spend a few hours in the morning setting up. Surprisingly no one has ever complained, even though we charge fifty cents for the carnival and some of our "games of skill" are things like Stand on a Chair and Drop a Penny in a Muffin Tin. The prizes are all old Happy Meal toys and other junk we've collected from the bottom of our toy boxes. Martin usually includes a sign saying *Play Till You Win!*, which means some kids stand on the chair for twenty minutes, dropping pennies. We also have beanbag throws with a cutout clown nose so small no one can ever win, so we have to give prizes for hitting the board at all, which makes it boring.

Last time, the most popular attraction was the Toddler Roller Coaster, which is basically a cardboard box Martin pushes up the hill in our backyard with a toddler in it, then he turns around and slides them back down. The kids loved laughing at Martin's sweaty face, and in the end, it made the most money.

Another moneymaker we've done is having a tag sale, where we bring out all our broken toys, lay them on a blanket, and try to talk all the little kids into buying everything that doesn't work anymore or wasn't fun to begin with.

I've also tried setting up a lemonade stand, where I sat for two hours beside the bus stop. Doing that, I learned that not everyone will feel sorry enough for a kid sitting by himself with a pitcher of lemonade to buy a cup. Some people will say, "What kind of lemonade?" and when you say "Crystal Light," they'll shake their heads. That day I lowered my price twice and still only made two dollars and fifty cents, which isn't very much for a long time of sitting. Finally Mom felt so sorry for me that she came out and paid me a dollar for a cup of lemonade she'd originally paid for herself. I don't think we should do that again.

Martin's trying to get ten items on the list, so I remind him of the small jobs we've done for neighbors. Every winter I offer my services knocking icicles off old people's porch roofs. This earns more money than you'd think, especially if you grunt while you do it and make it sound like hard work. I also pick up rotten crab apples in the fall, which can be messy and dangerous if there are bees underneath them. Sometimes I have to wear a catcher's mitt.

As I list these for him, Martin includes some of the regular jobs he does for neighbors: lawn mowing, dog walking, cat feeding.

"Here's the idea," he says when he's got ten items. "We're going to have a big block party carnival to benefit the Brian Barrows Medical Fund. We'll combine all these things. We'll have games and a tag sale. We'll have a bake sale table and ask people to bring things. We do a silent auction where people bid on certificates good for lawn mowing and all these other chores."

I'm surprised. Lawn mowing all spring and summer is Martin's main source of income for the year. Because he makes so much doing that, Mom doesn't give him an allowance anymore. "But that would be all your money."

"Yeah, true, but look at you. You were about to sell Spidey. This is the least I could do. Plus think about it. People want to help out—they just aren't too sure how, so they're raking our leaves and leaving all this food. The truth is, we don't really need the food anymore. This is what we need. And I'm telling you, people will totally overpay us for stuff this time around."

He laughs and writes down more ideas. "Thanksgiving's coming up! We'll make it a holiday carnival. We'll sell pumpkin pies and turkey place cards. We'll get a theme going."

"Turkey place cards?" Mom says when we tell her the idea over dinner that night. "You mean the folded pieces of paper with turkey stickers on them?" Mom makes new ones every year, so George, with his terrible handwriting, can have one job every year, writing everyone's name. "How much could you charge for those? A quarter? A nickel?"

Martin smiles. "Here's the best part of the whole idea." He holds up one hand like a movie director framing his shot. "No prices on anything. We'll make one sign that says, *Pay What You Want to Benefit Brian Barrows Medical Fund.*" Martin took a class in psychology this year as an elective. Now he thinks he knows everything about how humans think and what motivates people. He drops his hand, really smiling now. "If you don't tell them a price, they pay more. All the studies bear this out. People rip themselves off out of guilt. Or the fear of seeming cheap."

Mom shakes her head. "Martin, it's a nice idea, but I don't want to bring the whole neighborhood in on our problems. It feels a little desperate. I don't think we're desperate."

"Well, I mean I'm sorry, Mom, but we sort of are."

Mom looks at both of us.

"Look at it this way, Mom," Martin says. "We could try this or we could try something else. We could be the coffee-can family that collects change next to cash registers around town. Would you rather do that?"

"Okay," she finally says, smiling and wiping away a tear at the same time. "But we have to make sure it's a fun carnival for the kids. I don't want this to be a big pity party for the Barrows family."

"No way, Mom. Trust us," Martin says. "This'll be all about fun."

Which also means there's one thing everyone agrees on: Dad shouldn't come.

"It'll be way too overwhelming for him," Mom says. "Plus I don't want him to start worrying about all this money stuff. He's got enough on his plate just getting better."

She's right. And maybe there's something she doesn't want to say but we all know. Lisa isn't the only person Dad has been weird around. He's now spent the day with both sets of grandparents and both times he's cried in embarrassing ways. None of us could watch it, he looked so much like a kid. So, no. We love Dad and we're doing this for him, but we don't want him to be there, embarrassing himself and the rest of us.

But where can he go? The rehab center where he spends most of his weekdays isn't open on the weekend. Some people stay there all the time, but we can't check him in for nonmedical reasons, Mom says. She thinks about her two best friends, who have already been over. One is Polly, our old kindergarten teacher, who Mom says is like the sister she never had. When she came over, she sat next to Dad and didn't mind at all when he put his head on her shoulder and fell asleep for a few minutes.

"We'll just have Polly spend the day with him," Mom says. "She'll bring him over to her house. She'll be happy to do that. It'll be good for him actually. The doctors are saying we should alter his routine so he learns to adapt to schedule changes." She sounds like she could be talking about George.

Martin and I look at each other, but we don't say anything because there's too much to do and having a plan like this puts us all in a pretty good mood.

We need to start organizing the game part of the carnival. We need to start collecting old clothes and toys for the tag sale. We need to start baking a zillion pies that Martin thinks people will pay a lot for. It's funny. Now that Martin's being so nice about doing this so I don't have to sell my minifigs, I want to do a really great job. I want to have a real games arcade and design the best games I can think of. I want to bake great pies and have people say things like, "Here, why don't I give you fifty dollars for this pie." I keep imagining moments like that.

We spend a week getting ready. We pull out our old toys

and clothes. Martin gets some of his old friends to help, and I have to say I'm surprised. It's been years since I've seen most of them do anything besides play a video game, but now they all bring over their best old toys and on Friday we have a pile of Nerf guns in our living room that's higher than our coffee table.

"They all work, too," Martin says when he catches me staring at them.

I wonder if I could withdraw birthday money from the bank and buy them all up or if that would defeat the whole point of this fund-raiser.

"I look at that and I think a hundred bucks, easy," Martin says.

I have thirty in the bank so never mind.

Mom and George and I spend every afternoon making pies with homemade crusts, which is easy once you get the hang of it. By the end we have fourteen and have to stop because we have no room to hold any more.

Martin stares at the table on the screened porch where they're all laid out with little place cards on top, saying what kind they are. "I look at this and I'm thinking another hundred and twenty dollars easy."

When Mom looks surprised, he says, "You think anyone's

gonna give us *less* than eight dollars a pie?"

The Friday before our carnival is the last day of the C.A.R.E. footprints program. It turns out our class didn't win the pizza party. We didn't even come close. Ms. Shiner's fifth grade class won with sixty-seven footprints and we had only nineteen. Three for Jeremy, one each for almost everyone else. As Mr. Norris passes each person's footprint back to them, here is the biggest surprise: there are none for Rayshawn, who I think of as the nicest guy in our class.

I almost can't believe it. It makes me wonder if he really *was* inviting me to play basketball with him, not just trying to get a footprint. Because if Rayshawn cared about footprints, he would have one.

Mr. Norris tells us we should keep our footprints as important artifacts from this year (we just learned the word *artifact* in social studies a week ago), which makes them seem a little cooler, except I can't stop looking over at Rayshawn, who doesn't have one.

"You should have gotten about *five*," I whisper to him. "It's not *fair*."

"Nah," he says, smiling like I'm being funny. "What for?"

I look down at my footprint, which means a lot to me because it's one of the only ones with Mr. Norris's handwriting. I thought for sure I'd keep this in my special treasures drawer at home, but suddenly there's something I want to do with it more. I turn it over and write: *I appreciate how Rayshawn invites terrible players like Benny B. to play basketball at recess. Someday Benny B. might actually do it.*

When he turns around to get his math book out, I put the footprint on Rayshawn's desk.

Here's the best part—he laughs for about thirty seconds when he reads it. He laughs so hard his forehead touches his desk, then he looks back at me. "Thanks, man. I might just keep this," he says.

I watch him put it in his backpack and I think, *That feels better than getting the stupid thing myself.*

Maybe I really am growing up because that afternoon Mr. Norris reads us the last Zen short story and I sort of understand it. Or I think I do.

"Let's see what you think," he says ahead of time.

The story is about a mother whose baby has died. She is so sad she goes to Buddha and says she'll do anything to bring her baby back to life. Buddha says he'll grant her wish if she brings him a mustard seed from a house that has never known death. The woman accepts the challenge. She starts in her own village and then moves across the countryside, knocking on doors and asking strangers if anyone in their family has died. She figures out that every house has lost someone. The last line of the story explains the point the way a lot of the other ones haven't. "She loses the challenge but discovers a community to share her pain with."

When he finishes the story, Mr. Norris looks up at me. When he did this before, I wanted to say, *Don't look at me! I don't understand!* But this time it's a little different. This time I think I *do* understand it. I'm not sure I can put it into words, though. Just like he had a hard time writing up a footprint for me. George and Aaron aren't always easy to be around, but we still love them.

That's it, I guess. That's what we share.

When you put it into words it doesn't seem like much, but we both know it's a lot.

TWENTY-SIX

THE NIGHT BEFORE THE CARNIVAL IT'S hard to sleep because we have no idea what's going to happen. We've put flyers around town and a notice on our school's website calendar. I told Mr. Norris and Ms. Crocker and on Friday they made a joint announcement over the PA, which really surprised me.

At first I thought that was embarrassing, especially when Jeremy said, "What, like a *kiddie* carnival? Are you serious? We're in the fourth grade now, remember?"

Then a bunch of kids came up and said they wanted to come. Our house is on a pretty busy street, so it was easy to tell them where it was. Rayshawn said he'd come after basketball practice, which made me happy and nervous and exaggerate the number of Nerf guns we have for sale. ("There's like a hundred," I said. "Seriously. You should get some." He laughed like I was kidding, the way he always does.) At the end of the day, walking back from our math class, Olga asked if there were any jobs she could help with. I couldn't picture her helping little kids drop their pennies—I'm not sure if she could see a penny or the place they were aiming—so I said she was welcome to bring any old toys or desserts, or anything else she wouldn't mind selling.

The next morning we wake up to the first bad surprise of the day: Polly, my mom's friend, has shingles and can't take Dad to her house for the day. I think of shingles as the things on the roofs of houses but apparently it's also a very painful sickness. "It's fine," Mom says, blowing out in a way that makes me pretty sure it's not fine. "We'll set Dad up upstairs, with the TV on, and we'll check on him every half hour or so."

"Right," Martin says. "I'm sure that'll work. He won't wonder at all why there's a million people in the backyard."

For a second, Mom gets seriously mad. "I don't want him to know why we're doing this. He'll feel *terrible* if he knows this is about his medical bills. Promise you'll help me, boys."

We promise her and then, a few minutes later, we get the second surprise of the day: Olga shows up an hour early, bringing her own table and a box filled with her comic books. Each one has a cardboard cover and is stapled together with her drawings on the front.

"Are you sure you want to sell these?" I say. "Don't your parents want to save them or something?"

Because of their homemade covers, they look a little like the books I made back in kindergarten. My parents' favorite is still on display on our family room bookshelf. It has two pages: one with a picture of a hill with a face on it, the next with a sentence a teacher helped me write: *This is me, dressed up as a hill.* I remember my dad reading that one and saying, "Books don't get much better than this, Benny."

Olga lays her books out in a rainbow shape on her table. "These are all copies. We've got originals at home." She pulls out a coffee can with a sign taped to it: *Olga Yashenowitz Comic Series for Sale. All Profits to Benafit Benny's dad's Medicle Expenses.*

I know some of those words are misspelled, and I feel embarrassed for her and sorry that I said she could bring anything to sell. I should have been clearer. I should have said, *You can bring either old toys or desserts.* I can't help worrying that she'll sit here all day without selling a single book, because why would anyone want to *buy* a little kid's book?

Then I pick one of them up and I'm a little surprised. The graphics are great. The pictures are all divided into real panels with great drawings. I start to read the first one and I'm even more surprised. It's about a blind girl who discovers she has the superpower of going into other people's minds and changing what they think. At first she plays tricks with her power. She goes into minds of kids she doesn't like and makes them forget all the words on the spelling test. Then she makes everyone in the class fail a math test just so she'll look smart. In the end she realizes it's not that fun to be the smartest person in the class and that day at lunch, she goes into everyone's mind and makes them all share their lunches with one girl who forgot hers.

Okay, so it's not *The Indian in the Cupboard*, but it's good enough that I pick up the next one to see what happens. This time Blind Girl is trying to get strong enough to change grown-ups' minds. She works and works to get her parents to pick Disneyland for their next vacation instead of some boring historical site with battlefields and museums, which they always do. She almost does it. She hears her mother humming "It's a Small World" and then: Tragedy! Blind Girl breaks her arm! Her parents feel so bad about it they tell her she should pick their next vacation spot. Disneyland, here they come!

It's weird reading these because I remember Olga coming to school in second grade with a cast on her arm. Those were the days when boys really didn't talk to girls so I don't think I ever asked how she broke it.

Over the rest of the morning, when I'm not busy running my games arcade (which, I have to be honest, probably makes the least money of all our setups), I go over to Olga's table and keep reading her books. In one, Blind Girl goes to camp and saves a drowning boy by teaching his mind how to swim. In that one, Blind Girl also helps a friend at camp not be afraid of the dark. I like how Blind Girl controls people's thoughts. Usually she whispers something like *You can do this*. It makes me think about Olga with her fingers on her knees teaching me multiplication. I look over her titles and wonder if I'm in one of these books somewhere.

"You could buy one," she says, after I've read four. "But you don't have to. It's up to you."

A few people have bought some, but there's still a lot left.

Now that she's said this I realize I really want to. I want

the whole series. I want to figure out how she did this on the computer when she can't see print very well. I want to talk to her about making an animated movie version of one of these stories using one of my girl Lego minifigures like Poison Ivy or Cat Woman. Maybe she won't like that idea, but maybe she will.

I borrow money from my game arcade coffee can, which I can pay back with birthday money from the bank, and I go back to Olga's table. I offer to pay one dollar each for the first six books in the Blind Girl series. She pulls an already-tied-together stack of books out of a box at her feet and says, "Here you go. Put the money in the can."

After that, I watch her table and it turns out she's selling a lot more than it looks like—she's leaving the same ones on the table and pulling other copies out of the boxes under the table. One little kid gets done with my game circuit and asks if he can read the copies lying on my chair. "My sister bought them, but she won't let me look at them until she's done."

By this point we're getting a little busier, so I say fine. I've had about ten kids come through my game arcade, which isn't a lot but is enough to keep me busy. Overall we've had about forty people come, most of them to look over the tag sale and the bake sale. Then I look up the street where more cars are parked and—this freaks me out for a second—I see Mr. Norris and Ms. Crocker get out of his car, then open the back door so Aaron can get out.

I look around the yard and try to decide how this will look to them. A lot of people have come and gone. There's about twenty people right now, standing around in clusters. A line of parents and toddlers are at Martin's roller coaster, which is going even better this year because there are three vehicles (cardboard boxes) and two friends to help with the pushing that is everyone's favorite part. Even his friends have gotten into it, making sweaty faces while the babies laugh in their boxes.

Mom is at the pie table. It's loaded with things other people have brought, including zucchini breads that no one will buy probably and a huge chocolate chip cookie, frosted and shaped like a football, which I really want to buy with the rest of the money in my can (which I'll also have to pay back from my bank account).

George is meant to be "helping" Mom at the bake sale table, which means he's wandering around doing whatever he wants, which makes me even more nervous. I see Mr. Norris and Aaron walking up the street, coming closer.

Aaron is wearing another candy necklace. If it wasn't obvious by his outfit that there's something wrong with him, he's holding his dad's hand, which pretty much makes it clear. George still holds hands with our parents, too, even though he's in sixth grade. Not all the time though. They try to remind him holding hands is for street crossing, not walking around the grocery store.

The main thing is, I don't want George to run over and scare Aaron. I also don't want him to start screeching and making Aaron's noises back to him, thinking that's a good way to say hello. I can tell how nervous Mr. Norris is about bringing Aaron to our carnival.

When they first got out of the car, I assumed I was seeing something shocking, like next week he might announce that he and Ms. Crocker are getting married. I know that happens sometimes; teachers marry each other because who else do they meet? Watching them walk closer though, I'm not so sure. Ms. Crocker looks nervous, too, like she doesn't know Aaron and isn't sure what to do with him. That happens all the time with George. Nice people get really awkward if they don't know him. Which makes me think they're friends but probably not getting married anytime soon. She's here to help, because he wanted to bring Aaron and maybe he wasn't sure he could do it alone.

Aaron walks toward us, chewing on the hand that Mr. Norris isn't holding. It's hard to tell if he's hurting himself or not. But he's scared. I can tell.

All morning I've been wishing we had more people and a bigger crowd and now I wish there was no one else here. I bet I could get Aaron to do the Penny Drop if no one else was around. That would probably surprise Mr. Norris and make him happy.

I feel like running over to George and saying he has to go inside the house and not come out for at least half an hour. He's the one who's most likely to do weird, unpredictable things that might scare Aaron away. I leave my post and run over to Mom. "Mr. Norris is here! With Aaron! You have to get George inside." I'm trying to whisper and not seem hysterical, but I do anyway.

"Benny, I can't make George—" Mom says and then looks up and sees Mr. Norris and Aaron on the edge of the lawn. Aaron's up on his toes. It looks like he doesn't want to step on the grass. Mom takes it all in—the two adults trying to reassure Aaron, the big deal this is, just stepping on grass—and she says, "Okay, let me see what I can do."

She heads toward George, who's sitting on our old swing set, twirling himself around. Before she gets to him, though, something happens that makes everyone on the lawn turn around in the same direction.

I hear someone say, "Oh my God," and I look: Dad is standing on the back porch, wearing no hat or bandanna. His bald head shines in the sunlight; his scars look like train tracks across his forehead and over his ear. My stomach tightens. He is wearing a big smile, holding up one hand to wave, like he has no idea at all how scary he looks to all these people.

TWENTY-SEVEN

"BRIAN!" MOM CALLS. SHE HAS TO run over to him. Otherwise he might try to walk down the stairs and he can't do that without help. His depth perception is bad and one leg is so weak it buckles underneath him.

I know this is Mom's worst fear for today. She's worried about Dad but she's also worried about everyone seeing the truth about Dad and feeling sorry for us.

Now it's too late—people are waving and calling out hello.

"Oh, Brian! There you are," Carla, an old friend, calls out. "You look wonderful! Come down and say hello!"

Dad smiles and doesn't move. Mom is at the stairs, moving

up toward him. I look around at who's on the lawn and try to think. *How many people here know that he still can't talk?* These aren't our good friends. Our good friends came early and are already gone. The people here now are acquaintances and some strangers.

The worst would be if Dad gets caught up in the moment and forgets what he can't do. If he thinks, *Oh look, friends!* and comes down to spend twenty minutes trying to get *hello* to come out of his mouth.

George doesn't mind running up the stairs to stand next to Dad. Dad puts his arm around George and everyone waits for a long minute to see what will happen next. I have to say this—George and Dad look more related to each other now than they used to. Like they're more than just father and son now. They're two people who've been in the same car accident or something. They're both reeling away, trying to figure out what happened.

I'm not sure why Mom isn't climbing the stairs to do something. Maybe she's like the rest of us, waiting to see what Dad is going to do. Finally he smiles, squeezes George to his side, and holds up a big thumbs-up sign. George does it, too, and everyone claps.

Mom climbs the stairs and turns around to say, "Brian

just wants to thank everyone so much for coming out today. Our whole family appreciates this incredible show of support." She's crying as she says this, which makes me run over and stand next to her. "I mean that," she says, squeezing me. "We've learned a lot today about how generous people can be. We are so grateful to all of our friends who have helped us." She looks over at Olga, who is listening and counting her coffee can of money. It looks like she's made a lot.

Martin's friends at the toy sale whoop and hold up a fistful of dollar bills. I hadn't even noticed until now but all the Nerf guns are sold. And so are most of the other toys. *"Go, Mr. Barrows!"* one of them yells.

Dad raises his eyes and gives them another thumbs-up. It makes me wish I had a crowd of guy friends like Martin does. Rayshawn hasn't come, which means the only person I have here is Olga. Maybe she's my only friend, which shouldn't depress me, but it sort of does.

And then I look over at my station and see another surprise. Mr. Norris and Aaron and Ms. Crocker are all standing in the game arcade. He must know this is my spot because I made one of the games from the recycle bin in art class. It's a cardboard ball maze constructed with toilet paper rolls stapled onto a piece of cardboard. It's my favorite game in the arcade even if no one has played it yet.

I come over and say hello to Mr. Norris and Ms. Crocker and offer Aaron a high five, which is the only way George will say hi to strangers. Aaron does it, sort of, only he misses my hand.

Mr. Norris and Ms. Crocker tell me it looks like a great fair and a great game arcade. They keep talking, but I don't listen too closely because I'm looking at what Aaron is studying: our old beanbag toss game with the clown nose that's too small.

I pick up a beanbag and show him how, even if you stuff it, it's hard to get through. I'm surprised because I've got his attention. He's definitely watching. When I finally get the beanbag to disappear through the nose, he does something George would totally do: he laughs really loud.

I reach around with my other hand and pull the beanbag out again. "Ta-da!" More laughter!

Stuff it through: he laughs.

Make it reappear: he laughs again.

I do it a bunch of times and then I change it up a little. I hand the beanbag to him. He doesn't take it. He pushes my hand toward the hole, so I'll keep doing the trick. This is just like George, who will pull me over to the refrigerator to get me to open the door for him. He knows how to do things, he just doesn't think he *can*. "You do it," I say, holding the beanbag out to Aaron.

He puts his fingers in his ears like he's trying to say, *No, don't say that. You do it.*

I do it a few more times so he's laughing again and the fingers are out of his ears. Then I take a risk: I just put the beanbag in his hand.

He doesn't want to do it himself, but he wants the game to keep going, so it's almost like his hand does it by itself. He pushes the beanbag through and laughs. I pull it out. "Ta-da!" And he laughs again. He does it again and we crack ourselves up.

We've got a pretty good joke going that reminds me of playing around with George, where nothing you're doing is all that funny and you laugh just because the other person is laughing so hard.

The game ends when I see my fourth big surprise of the day: Jeremy pushing his bike across the lawn. He looks mad, like he's already been to the toy sale and found out all the Nerf guns are gone. Maybe he's figured out this is Mr. Norris's son I'm standing with. Maybe he saw Mr. Norris put a twenty-dollar bill in my coffee can, which he did a few minutes ago. I wave to Jeremy, nervous about what he might say. "Hi! Thanks for coming!"

"Are people supposed to pay for these games?" he says.

Aaron has already walked away, so it's fine for me to talk to him. I look around at what he's seeing. Each game is balanced on a plastic lawn chair. It looks pretty stupid. "Yeah, but not too many people have. Mostly they're doing the other stuff."

"I can see why."

I want to tell him he should try to sound less mean. Maybe it would even help him if I pointed this out, but I'm not so sure. He looks over at Olga, sitting at her table. "Are you pretty good friends with her now?"

"I guess." I shrug. "You should look at her books. They're pretty good."

He doesn't go over there.

Part of me wishes he would just leave.

At least my dad is back inside and George went with him, so I don't have to worry about either of them. But there's some people who can make you feel embarrassed about everything in your life, even things like your lawn or your swing set.

Then I'm really surprised. Jeremy rolls his bike over to the tree next to my arcade and lays it on the ground. "Maybe I could help you," he says. "You need to get people over here. How about if I be your barker?"

"What's that?"

"The guy at the circus who shouts at people to get them to buy things."

"You want to do that?"

He shrugs. "Sure. I don't mind."

A few minutes later, he's rolled up some extra poster board paper to make a megaphone and he's shouting, "All right, everyone! There's a game arcade over here that no one's going to, but it's pretty fun. The price is right because it's pay whatever you want, and you can win some prizes!"

Some people standing near him look like they're not sure if he's joking or not.

"Right over here, sir. You, on the grass next to the swing set. It might not look like too much, but it's a homemade game arcade and you should bring your kids over to try it. This might be the only chance they ever get to play in a ball maze made out of toilet paper rolls. It's something they'll tell their grandkids, and their grandkids will get confused, like, wait, wasn't there electricity then, so why the toilet paper rolls? Just go, sir. You with the Red Sox shirt on. Go. Seriously."

I look over at my mom, who is laughing harder than I've seen her laugh in a long time. The man starts laughing, too, and shuffles his kids over in my direction.

Jeremy keeps going, using his megaphone to talk to people standing five feet away from him. When my area fills up with little kids dropping pennies and throwing beanbags, he starts selling the other areas.

"You, sir, in the orange jacket! You look like maybe you need some new comic books in your life."

Olga has never liked Jeremy much. Not that she's said it, but I can tell from the way she looks at him over her glasses and usually rolls her eyes. This time though, I'm surprised. She laughs and holds some of her sample books up high. *"Right over here!"* she yells louder than I've ever heard her speak in five years.

TWENTY-EIGHT

JEREMY KEEPS US BUSY FOR THE rest of the afternoon. When Rayshawn walks up and asks if he's too late, Jeremy shouts through his megaphone, "Too late? Are you kidding? We're just getting started."

Rayshawn is still wearing his basketball clothes so he doesn't have any pockets or any money. Instead of buying anything he comes over to the game arcade and helps me with the three little kids I have playing the games. He does a great thing at the beanbag toss, where he tells them to forget the clown and try to hit him. Then he dances around and makes it really hard. The kids laugh so hard and stay so long at the game, the dad puts another five dollars in my can.

Considering it's a terrible game that doesn't work very well, we've had a pretty good time at the beanbag toss this year.

After it's all over, Mom hugs all my friends and invites them inside to count our money and eat the one pie that's left over, strawberry rhubarb.

"No offense, Ms. Barrows," Jeremy says. "But there might be a reason that pie is left over."

My mom laughs again and tells Jeremy he should be a comedian. I've never thought about it this way, but maybe Mom is right. Maybe all the things he says that have made me feel bad weren't insults but were jokes.

Olga says she'd love to stay and find out how much money we made but she's allergic to gluten so no thank you on the pie. George, who has come back outside and is bouncing in a circle near us, comes straight over to Olga.

"You're allergic to gluten?" he says. We're all surprised. Usually George doesn't listen in on conversations unless we force him to. "I'm allergic to gluten, too."

Olga's eyes shake a little when she tries to look at him, which George loves. He stares right into her weird, shaky eyes. It's the first time I've ever seen him make perfect eye contact.

"It sucks sometimes, doesn't it?" she says.

George bounces away with an excited laugh. "It sucks!" he says and then repeats the whole sentence a few more times into his hand. It didn't last very long, but I look at Mom and I can tell she's thinking the same thing: it seems like George tries to be a tiny bit more normal around girls. This isn't saying much because he's still pretty far from normal, but maybe it's a start.

First Lisa, now this.

Maybe he is changing.

It turns out we made the most money at the bakery table, where the adults were congregated and a few people donated hundred-dollar checks and took a pie as a thank-you. Mom felt pretty embarrassed about that, but Martin told her that was the whole point, so she should stop feeling embarrassed. The next surprise was that Olga made the second most—seventy-two dollars. "My goal was seventy-five," she said, shaking her head. "But I got close."

Seventy-five dollars?? I thought. It reminded me of something Dad used to say: *You'll be very surprised by which kids in your class end up being the most successful grown-ups.* I used to assume it would be Jeremy but maybe not.

"Olga, we thank you so much for donating your day and

all your books to this effort," my mom says. "It was very generous of you."

Olga shrugs and her eyes shake. "It's okay. I liked it."

Martin comes over and surprises everyone by putting his arm around Olga and giving her a kiss on the cheek. "You're cool, Olga," he says. "A very cool girl." I'm pretty sure he's doing this because Mary Margaret is here and he's in a good mood. He told me last week that he finally talked to her about how he felt. They're not boyfriend and girlfriend yet but they're hanging out more and next week they're going to a movie together.

Olga blushes and scratches her face so hard her glasses tip to the side of her nose. "I don't know about *that*," she says.

Mom doesn't forget to thank Jeremy and Rayshawn. "I'm pretty sure you two are responsible for doubling Benny's haul at the game arcade." She's right. I had about twenty-four dollars when Jeremy came over. Now I have fifty-seven. They both look happy about that and I can't help it—I'm happy that Martin isn't the only one with friends who don't mind coming over and helping out.

When we add everything up, including the silent auction donations people sent who couldn't come, we have more than six hundred dollars. We're all amazed.

"And you still have your Lego dudes," Martin whispers.

He's right. I do.

It all feels great. Then Dad wanders in to smile at the pile of money and then at all of us.

We got through the earlier moment that Mom was so scared of and now I can see how nervous she is. As she sweeps up the money, Dad tugs on my shirt and hands me a note. My heart starts to beat so fast I can feel it in my stomach.

I don't want to read his note.

I don't want to ruin the nice day we've just had.

But everyone saw him hand it to me and everyone wants to know what it says. I don't want to read it. "It's okay," Mom says.

I shake my head. I can't read it. I'll cry if I have to read it.

"Dude, Dad's trying to tell you something," Martin says. "Just read it."

Martin doesn't know what Dad's been asking me to do. He doesn't know that Dad's brain is stuck in a groove it can't get out of. Suddenly it's like all the happy feelings inside me turned into mad ones. *"No!"* I scream. *"I'm not going to!"*

I have to leave the room because if I don't, Olga, Jeremy, and Rayshawn, my only three friends in the world, will see me cry. They'll know I'm not just stupid, I'm uncoordinated, too. I'm a fourth grader who's terrible at multiplication *and* bike riding. Which is another way of saying if the rest of my family didn't have huge problems, I'd be the one everyone is worried about. Because even Dad, who's got a lot of problems, is more worried about me than he is about himself.

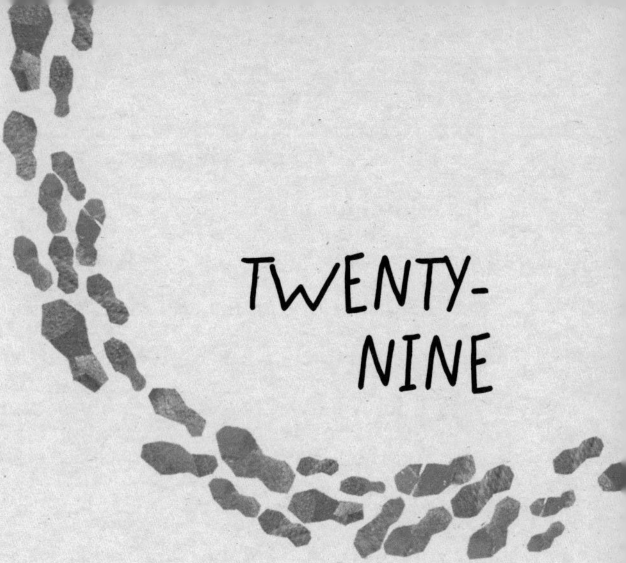

TWENTY-NINE

I DON'T EVEN SAY GOOD-BYE TO MY friends, I just disappear up to my room after that. When Mom comes in later and sits down on the edge of my bed, I start crying.

"You know what I'm starting to think?" Mom says.

"What?"

"I'm thinking maybe we should all just go to the track tomorrow. Maybe Dad needs this for some reason. Maybe it's not a terrible idea."

Just the idea of getting on a bike again scares me and makes me start crying again. "I don't want more bad things to happen."

"They won't, baby. I promise. Nothing bad will happen."

"What if we do it and he just keeps suggesting it? What if this is his thing now?"

"Then we'll figure out a way to get him off it." She puts her arms around me and kisses the top of my head. "I watched you today with Mr. Norris's son. You were so good with him. The way you figured out a game he wanted to play and then got him to play it with you. There aren't too many kids your age who could do that."

"You think Dad might want to play beanbags instead of bike riding?"

"No," she says. "I think if we listen to Dad and do this for him, we might figure out what he's after and get him to move on. That's what I hope anyway."

"I just keep being scared. I can't help it. I don't know why. It's stupid."

"It's not stupid. It's scary because bad things can happen so suddenly. But it wasn't bike riding or your accident that made Dad have his aneurysm. That was going to happen sooner or later anyway. I think our whole lives we've been getting ready for this. George helped us and we didn't even realize it."

"So we have to do it? We have to go bike riding?"

"Yes," she says. "I think we have to do it."

★ ★ ★

The next morning, everyone tiptoes around me like I'm a crazy bomb that might go off any second. Martin is already sitting at the breakfast table, eating cereal out of a salad bowl. When I sit down, he nudges the almost-empty box of Cocoa Krispies toward me. Then he looks up, and gasps. I look over and see: Dad is standing there wearing his old jogging shorts and his terrible terry cloth wristbands we haven't seen in more than four months.

Under his breath, I hear Martin say, "Oh my God."

Mom comes in a minute later, wearing yoga pants and sneakers. Her hair is up in a ponytail. "Dad thinks we should all go to the track this morning! I do, too! It's a beautiful day—we'll have fun."

We're all putting on a show that no one told Martin about. Finally he says, "Ah, Mom, are we allowed to talk about this?"

"I'd rather not," Mom says, clapping her hands. "I'd rather just go."

Martin stands up and walks over to her. "Seriously, Mom," he whispers over her shoulder. "This is a joke, right?"

"Not at all. Go put on some shorts, Martin. It won't kill you to run around the track a little. Benny and George can bring their bikes. Come on, guys. Up and at 'em."

An hour later, we're all at the track, with Lucky bouncing around on the leash Martin's holding. Mom has packed a cooler of water and snacks, and Martin can't walk and text on his new phone, so he's sitting in a patch of shade under a tree in the distance. Earlier I heard them having a fight in the pantry about this. Martin said it was a weird, stupid idea going back to a place where something so terrible happened. "What's the point, Mom?" he whispered because he didn't want me to hear, I'm pretty sure. "It'll just make Benny feel like crap. We had a nice day yesterday. Give it a rest."

"I can't give it a rest. Dad doesn't want to give it a rest. He wants to do this."

"Dad isn't exactly thinking so clearly these days, right? So maybe we don't need to do every bad idea he has."

Their voices were getting a little louder like maybe Martin didn't even care if I overheard or not.

"Don't ruin everything that was nice about yesterday. I don't care if you come with us or not. The four of us are going to the track because Dad has been asking Benny to do this for a long time. I don't know why. Maybe he wants to replace a bad memory with a good one. We're doing it because for whatever reason, Dad needs it. That's all. Period. End of discussion."

I didn't think Martin was going to come at all, but then at the last minute he started walking with us, reading something on his phone so he didn't have to say anything about it. Mom smiled but didn't say anything either.

Now she lines George and me up on the start line, which is a bad idea because George doesn't like races, even one he's sure to win because he can ride a bike and I can't.

"On your marks!" Mom says, way too loud.

"Come on, Mom," I say. "Can't we just ride?"

"Get set!"

I watch George to see what he does to start off and get going in a straight line.

Typical George—he's not even looking ahead or down at his bike. He's staring straight *up*—to the sky—and doing the impossible: balancing on his pedals without touching the ground or pedaling. He looks like a circus act. If he was anyone else, I'd say he was showing off, but I don't think George understands the idea of showing off.

"And go!"

George goes.

He's off and pedaling so fast, I don't even bother riding because it's too much fun watching him. He doesn't look where he's going because it doesn't matter, he can fly over the bumpy grass no problem. He even takes the corner of a long-jump pit, which is all sand and would have toppled most bike riders, but not George. He sends a spray of sand, keeps riding.

I don't know how a kid who can't tie his shoelaces or dribble a basketball can be so good at bike riding. It's like he's not even thinking about it. He's staring up at the sky and letting his body do the work while his mind is somewhere else.

Maybe that's the secret.

Out of the corner of my eye, I see Martin hold up his new phone as a camera. He takes a picture first of George, and then of me. *Don't!* I think. And then I can't help it, I want him to get a picture of me looking like George—flying free around the track, my head thrown back.

So I do it exactly like George did. I scream a little as I take off. I roll over grass and back onto the track. I pump my legs and stand up. I open my mouth and stick my tongue out. I close my eyes and put my head back.

It feels great. Somewhere behind, I hear Dad whoop and laugh. Mom is clapping and screaming, *"Go, Benny!"*

George and I ride for a while, doing laps and hooting every time we pass Dad. George rides for a while with his feet off the pedals and his legs sticking out. Then, like he's just thought of something, he stops his bike and stands for a second, looking up the street. I stop mine to see what he's looking at.

I can't believe it.

It's Lisa Lowes walking her dog toward us.

If anyone has the power to ruin this moment, it's Lisa. The last time she saw our whole family together, she burst into tears. It made us all feel terrible, like spending time with our family would always be hard for other people. Now I wonder if the same thing will happen. It makes me so nervous I want to run up the street and tell her to turn around before she gets here.

I also have to admit this. A little part of me is happy to see her, too.

I want her to see George and me riding bikes. I want her to see Mom and Dad sitting in the grass, smiling like (almost) normal people again. I want her to understand (somehow) that it was mean what she did—crying in front of our dad and then not caring at all about George going missing.

So I don't say anything. She starts running on the track like she's listening to her music and doesn't even see us. But even though she doesn't see us, we all see her. Martin shoots a look at Mom like he wants to say, *See, I told you what a bad idea this was.*

Even Dad looks nervous, maybe about Lisa or maybe just a woman running with a dog on a leash makes him finally remember what happened. He makes a sound that scares Mom enough to put her arm around him.

I do the only thing I can think of—I turn my bike around and walk it off the track. "Come on, George, let's go. We're done," I say. We can't leave before Lisa makes it around to us but maybe we can pretend we don't see her.

Except George can't pretend. He won't move. He's smiling and waiting for her to get closer. He wants her to see him and then he'll ride away from her, too nervous to speak to her probably. "Let's go, George," I whisper. "Now."

He doesn't budge.

"Come on, George," Martin says, coming up behind us. "We're leaving *now*."

I'm surprised at how scared Martin sounds. Even Mom, who usually wouldn't put up with running away from an awkward situation, is standing up, holding her hand out to Dad to get him moving.

It's strange to realize this: we're all scared of Lisa. Of how we once liked her and how bad she made each of us feel. The problem is, we can't move fast enough. Dad gets dizzy standing up and can't walk, even with Mom holding his arm. And George won't move, which means I'm stuck beside him as Lisa runs toward us.

Martin leans in. "Seriously, people. *Let's go.*"

It's too late.

George is holding up his hand. *"What are you guys doing here?"* he shouts. This is his new version of repeating: telling people what he wants them to say. He did it outside Mr. Norris's apartment and now he's doing it again.

Lisa looks up. She really didn't see us earlier because she's obviously surprised. "Hi, Martin," she calls, like she doesn't even see me or George. Like George wasn't the one who said something first.

"Hi, Lisa," he says nervously. "We were just leaving."

She stops running and stares at him. "So go," she finally says.

George is still smiling. He doesn't understand how this is painful for everyone. He's happy to see the pretty girl he remembers eating dinner with us a few times. At least that's what I assume.

I assume George doesn't understand what's going on here.

And then he does something so surprising, it's hard to be

sure what he understands and what he doesn't. He turns to Martin and takes the phone out of his hand. He drops his bike on the ground so he can walk over to Lisa, holding out the phone.

"George, what are you—" Martin's obviously worried that George feels some need to give Lisa his phone.

"Take our picture?" George says.

Usually George doesn't care about pictures unless it's Halloween. But he must remember Martin taking pictures a few minutes ago. Maybe he's just thought of this out of the blue.

But here's the weird part. It works.

"All of you?" she says doubtfully.

"Yes," Mom says loudly, walking over, holding Dad's hand. "All of us. Thank you, Lisa. That would be very nice of you." She puts a little emphasis on the word *nice*, like maybe Lisa needs help remembering what it means.

We group together, all of us around me and my bike.

"Smile!" Lisa says.

And we do.

Acknowledgments

Many thanks to the administration and staff at Crocker Farm Elementary School in Amherst, Massachusetts, who started "Footprints" as part of a schoolwide positive behavioral support program. I so loved following that line of footprints up the hallway that by the time I got to the end, I wanted to write a story about it. (Thanks especially to Derek Shea, Mike Morris, and Susan McQuaid, who took time to talk to me a little bit about it.)

This book had a long journey to publication and a champion in my old friend Jeanne Birdsall, whose kindness and generosity are a gift to so many fellow writers and every child who has been lucky enough to see her on a school visit. In addition, I am endlessly grateful to Tara Weikum, Chris Hernandez, and the whole team at HarperCollins, especially Kate Jackson, Gina Rizzo, and Elizabeth Ward, and to Margaret Riley King, who have been such wonderful supporters of all my books.

Last but not least, this book is closer to my real family than any other I've written, and I'm so grateful to Mike, Ethan, Charlie, and Henry for not minding the way I've borrowed some of their games, talk, and Lego-movie ideas and pretended they were my own.

Don't miss this heartwarming and humorous novel from Cammie McGovern!

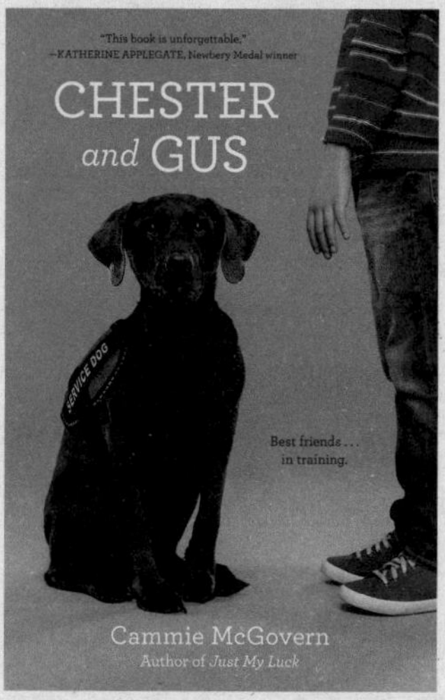

How to Tell Time

I'VE LIVED IN MY NEW HOME for three days but I still haven't met the boy I'm supposed to be best friends with.

He's nervous, I think.

So am I.

I don't know very many boys. I played with one once in the park where Penny brought me so I could get used to little children pulling on my fur and grabbing my tail. The boy in the park threw a ball and then a stick for me to fetch. When he got tired of that game, he said he was going to show me something called a slide that would be the most fun thing I'd ever done in my whole life. He picked me up and carried me to the top of it.

It was *not* fun. It was the opposite of fun. It was the most scared I've ever been except for the first time Penny practiced the "Dog Left Alone" test and tied me to a post for two minutes while she walked away. Afterward, she told me I wasn't supposed to whine or bark or show any signs of anxiety, which I didn't know at the time because I whined and barked like crazy. I couldn't help it. I was so anxious. This is what happens when you're a puppy. Your brain is so busy, you lose track of someone for a second and you think, *I haven't seen her for hours. She's probably dead.* You don't even know what dead is and you think it.

It's embarrassing now when I look back on it. I got nervous over lots of things back in those days.

When Penny came back, I dribbled pee I was so relieved to see her again! She knelt down and said, "It's okay, Chester. I was only gone two minutes," and I thought, *Really? Was it only two minutes? It felt more like two hours.*

I've never had a great sense of time and back then I wasn't completely sure what those words meant. Now I know. Two minutes is about the same as in a sec, and an hour means dinner's not for a long, long time, possibly days.

I loved our time at the park until that day the big boy carried me to the top of a slide and pushed me down. After that, I didn't love our trips to the park anymore.

Work

I KNOW I SHOULDN'T COMPLAIN ABOUT MY new home or this boy I haven't seen yet. It's my fault that I'm here, living with people who don't know their son very well if they got him a dog that he doesn't want to meet.

I was meant to be a service dog like my mother. She was a guide dog for a blind man until she got hit by a car, and then she retired to be a mother. "Being a mother is an important job, too," she told us, but she didn't really mean it. Having puppies made her tired and not very happy. Thinking about her old job made her happy.

"There's no better feeling than knowing there's one person in the world who depends entirely on you," she told us once. We were still small then and lying in a heap on top of each other. I had my brother Hershey's ear in my mouth. We all stopped what we were doing and listened.

"You meet your person and you *connect*. You learn what that person needs and you do it for them. It's the most satisfying feeling in the world."

After that we tried harder to pay attention during our puppy trainings. My sister Cocoa asked every person who gave us kibble or a drink of water, "Are you my person? Are *you*?"

Cocoa wasn't the smartest puppy in our litter. She was always eating things she wasn't supposed to.

One morning after breakfast, I looked up and saw a big group of people walking up the driveway of our farm. A few of them rolled in wheelchairs. One wore dark glasses.

Our people! I thought. *There they are!*

I ran to Cocoa and told her to come quick and look, but she was trying to eat a pinecone and didn't want to. My brother Hershey walked with me to the edge of our play yard and watched the group for a while.

Finally he said, "I want the big man in the rolling chair with pictures on his arms. You can have any of the others."

My heart started to beat faster. I didn't know how this worked—if we got to pick them or if they picked us. "Do we know enough yet to be paired with our person?" I asked.

"Yes," Hershey said. He was the biggest in our litter and

acted like he knew everything. "This is how it goes. Tomorrow we'll start our jobs. Remember, the man with pictures on his arms is mine."

For the rest of the morning, I worried. I thought about our mother's stories of her life with the blind man. *I did everything for Donald. I opened doors, I pressed elevator buttons, I guided him through traffic. Yes, I got hit by a car, but the important thing is: He didn't.*

There was so much I didn't understand. What was an elevator? What was traffic?

In the afternoon, we watched the people come outside with a group of dogs who were all wearing blue vests on their backs. Our mother came over to watch with us. When we pestered her with questions—*What are they wearing? What are they doing?*—she told us to be quiet.

"Just watch," she said. "This is the most important afternoon of their lives. They're being chosen by their person."

For the next hour, we watched them do tricks.

"Beautiful," our mother whispered under her breath. "Just beautiful."

"Sheesh," my brother Milton said softly. "That doesn't look like much fun."

"Fun isn't the point," Hershey snapped. "The point is getting someone to choose us."

I looked over at Hershey—his ears set forward, his nose working, taking it all in. I knew what he was thinking: *I want to wear a blue vest. I want to be chosen.*

I felt it too. We all did.

After the group went inside, we asked our mother more questions. "Learning all that will be the hardest thing you've ever done. You'll live with a trainer for almost a year and work constantly. That's all I can tell you. Even after all that work, some of you won't make it. That's just how it is."

She turned around and went back to her bed. That was that.

None of us knew what to think. Cocoa couldn't stop crying. "I don't want to *work hard.* I don't want to leave our play yard."

Milton was nervous, too. "What if we can't learn all those things?" By the end of the demonstration, the dogs were doing amazing things—finding and picking up tiny objects in the grass, holding a cane steady for someone who'd dropped it. "What if we can only learn about half those tricks?"

Hershey quieted him. "This is what we were born to do. It's our calling."

Cocoa whined some more.

"Don't be a crybaby," Hershey snapped.

In the middle of the night, I woke up and realized Cocoa was missing from our pile. I got the others up to help me look. We found her at the far end of our yard, lying on her side and moaning in pain, too sick to stand up. After Wendy, from the farmhouse, wrapped her up in a blanket and took her to the vet, our mother explained, "She ate three rocks last night. I have no idea why."

For a week we didn't see Cocoa, but we learned what the word "surgery" meant when Wendy told one of the workers: "Two hours of surgery. She had to have her stomach cut open and the rocks taken out."

When she finally came back, Cocoa seemed like a different dog—not really a puppy anymore.

A week later, she was given away.

"It's okay," our mother said, after she was gone. "Some dogs aren't cut out for the working life." She sounded as if we should all just forget about Cocoa for now.

I didn't of course. How could I?

Meeting Penny

HERSHEY WAS THE FIRST ONE TO be picked by a trainer and leave the farm. He didn't even look back as he got into the man's car. It was like he'd already forgotten his dog family, he was so ready to move on to the working part of his life.

After that, each of my brothers and sisters left one by one. I asked my mother if I should be worried that no trainer had picked me yet. "I don't know," she said. "Probably."

She wasn't a big one for reassuring her puppies. She didn't see the point. "Some of you won't make it as working dogs. That's all there is to it."

She didn't say Cocoa's name, but I thought of her of course.

After the last of my littermates was taken away and it

was just the two of us, my mother said, "They might think you're too much of a worrier." She snapped at a fly and went over for some water. "Try not to act so nervous the next time a trainer comes."

A few days later, I had my chance. Penny walked into our yard and right over to me. She wore a funny green hat and shoes with plastic flowers attached to them. "Look at you!" she said, reaching out to pick me up. "They must have saved the best for last!"

I wriggled and squealed and acted like a puppy again. I was so happy to be chosen I almost left without saying goodbye to my mother. At the last minute, I went over to the bed where she slept by herself now. "I have my trainer!" I said. "I'll see you in eight months! I'll work hard, you'll see! I'll try not to be too nervous, I promise!"

She confused me then, waking up from her nap, blinking at the light. "All right," she said. "I suppose it's too late now for anything else."

In the car, Penny told me all about herself. "Dogs are my true love, Chester. That's the first thing you should know about me. I've got no husband and no kids. Just a lot of wonderful dogs who I love and train and then I take them back to the farm to be matched with their person."

At her house, she showed me pictures of the dogs from her past in frames around her living room. Some of them looked like me in other colors, like yellow and black. "I've never had a chocolate lab like you. I think that's going to make you a little different from the rest."

She smiled as she said it and pulled me into her lap. I'd known her only a few hours and already she was nicer than my mother had ever been.

How to Be Understood

"EVERY DOG HAS A WEAKNESS," PENNY told me a few weeks into my training. "They're perfect in many ways and then suddenly, they see a rabbit in the woods and all their training goes out the window. Poof, off they go. If it's not a rabbit, it'll be something else. The trick is to figure out your challenge as early as possible, then work on it *a lot.* I've got a shelf full of windup squirrels if we need them."

I loved the way Penny talked to me all the time. I always answered, hoping she would understand me. *No thanks,* I tried to tell her that time. *I don't think squirrels will be my problem. I've seen lots of squirrels. I know not to chase them.*

I thought of what my mother had said and I wanted to be

honest with Penny. I looked her in the eyes. *I'm a little anxious sometimes. It might be a problem.*

She looked back at me and smiled reassuringly. "It's okay," she said, and for a second, I thought: *She understands! She knows what I'm saying!* Then she stood up. "I'm going to get one of those squirrels right now and try it on you."

A few days later, we discovered my weakness. After the boy carried me to the top of the slide. Penny worried that I might get scared of children, so she brought me to a school one morning and we sat outside the front door, saying hello to all the students as they walked in.

I was fine! Children were sweet! One girl lifted my ear and whispered, "You're the cutest dog in the whole world." Another girl lifted my other ear and said, "I love you!"

I love you too! I tried to say, but she didn't understand.

"No yipping, Chester," Penny said firmly, with a flat hand on my nose. It didn't hurt but still, I felt embarrassed. I had to remember that I understood what people said, but they couldn't understand me. I went back to the girls and licked their hands.

That's when it happened.

A terrible sound ripped through the air. My legs went jittery and frantic. I scrambled to get under a bench. *The sky is falling! The earth is blowing up!* I screamed to Penny, but she didn't hear me. How could she with all that noise?

When the noise finally stopped, I peeked out from the bench I was hiding under. I couldn't believe it. The children weren't scared at all! They even moved toward the door where the sound had come from.

After they were gone, Penny walked over to my hiding spot and crouched down. "That was just a school bell, silly dog. It looks like maybe loud sounds might be a problem, doesn't it?"

She talked softly to me the whole drive home. She told me it would be okay, that noises might hurt my ears but they couldn't hurt my body. She let me ride in the front seat next to her again, where she could keep a hand on my back. I was still having trouble catching my breath.

Her hand felt nice. So did her voice.

"We'll practice, that's all. When you don't expect it, I'll bang a few pots and pans and you'll get used to it. Caramel had this problem, too—you remember I told you about her? She got over it eventually."

That night while I ate my dinner, Penny dropped a cookie sheet on the floor. I thought it was a bolt of lightning hitting the house. I flew out of the room and under the sofa.

"Oh dear," Penny said from the kitchen. "Looks like we've got some work to do, Chester."

After that, we worked on it all the time. Along with heeling and fetching and opening doors, Penny and I practiced loud sounds. She whistled. She set off timers. Once, she deliberately set off her smoke alarm. She even warned me ahead of time as she held the match under the alarm. "This is going to be loud, sweetheart."

It was and I panicked. I knew I wasn't supposed to. Penny had told me many times: "When a loud sound comes, sit down and wait. Don't hide. Breathe in and out until it passes. Your person will need you. They have to be able to find you when it's over."

I knew all this and I still panicked. I couldn't help it. I ran as fast as I could and got under the closest bed or table I could find.

Except for this problem, my training went well. Almost every day, Penny told me how smart I was. One time, I knew what to do for a trick before she'd even taught me. The trick was opening a drawer and getting out a pot holder. It wasn't hard. I'd watched a dog do it on a DVD, but Penny must have forgotten, because after I brought it to her she said, "You might just be the smartest dog I've ever had."

After that, she did experiments to test my "vocabulary."

She put different objects around the room and asked me to fetch one without pointing at what she wanted.

"Please bring me my car keys, Chester," she'd say, and I could. That was easy because Penny misplaced them so much. Whenever she found them, she said, "I hate you, car keys! You always walk away!" I learned the word for "shoes" the same way and also "cell phone." Once she started those tests, I worked harder to remember the names of things because it made her so happy when I did.

It didn't seem like that much of an accomplishment to me until I heard Penny on the telephone with Wendy from the farm. "I've never seen such a young dog with such a big vocabulary. There are about fifty words that he's picked up entirely on his own. And it's not just that. He's six months old and he's already got so many commands down—heel, sit-stay, crate, go now, and don't touch."

Listening to Penny made me feel good.

"I've never seen a dog like this," she said. "He's remarkable, really. There's only one weak spot, I'd say. He seems to have a bit of sound sensitivity."

Those two words weren't in my vocabulary back then, but now they are.

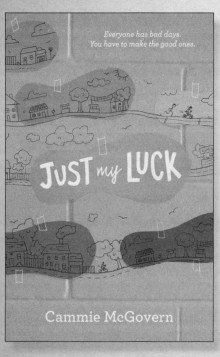

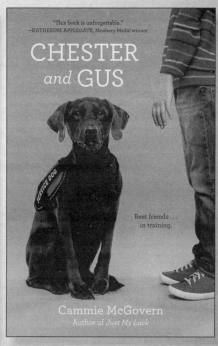